REDFERNE

by

Maurice Connolly

REDFERNE

First Published in 2006

Copyright © Maurice Connolly

ISBN-10: 0-9554620-0-2
ISBN-13: 978-0-9554620-0-9

Published by Goldenstown Books,
Foulksmills, Co. Wexford, Ireland
Telephone: 087 1332758
E-mail: sparianco@eircom.net

Printed by:
Modern Printers, Loughboy Industrial Estate, Kilkenny
Tel: 056-7721739

Grant me a sense of humour, Lord,
The saving grace to see a joke,
To win some happiness from life,
And pass it on to other folk.

Chapters

REDFERNE

Chapter One

Plan is Hatched

The townland is Redferne, near Dungarvan, Co. Waterford, Ireland. The location is a small farmhouse, isolated down a winding laneway. The laneway has formed a semi-arch as a down of whitethorn, ivy, furze and bracken lean inwards from both sides. Gentle hills surround the house and slope down to a small lake on the west side. The farm itself is small, consisting of thirty one acres. The fields, in a patchwork maze, making up this thirty one acres are also small – of the three to four acre variety. Each field is cherished, has a name, such as 'The Lake Field,' Jim's Field,' 'The Brow Field,' 'The Lawn,' and so on. It is a beautiful, warm, calm, balmy evening in mid-summer.

There aren't too many dwellings in the immediate area. There is a neglected, derelict house at the entrance to the lane, the owners having long-since emigrated to the States. Some newly erected bungalows – displaying a new source of wealth in the countryside – are visible in the distance. The Celtic Tiger has arrived in Ireland.

The inside of the farmhouse hasn't changed much down the years. Piped water has been made available and a bathroom has been installed. Other than that, everything has, more or less, remained the same. The old Aga cooker is still working away in the kitchen, the same as it has done for the past thirty years. The cooker itself gives out a degree of heat, but the traditional open fireplace with fan, is still used. A strong kitchen table with chairs occupies the centre of the room. Framed photographs of family members, most of whom are deceased, adorn the walls. A cupboard, displaying chinaware, is situated at the back wall. The kitchen sink and wall cabinets are located to the left of the two front windows. A fridge and television are also in evidence.

Outside in the farmyard some free-range chickens are scratching about. A black and white collie dog, rolled up in a fluffy ball, has settled down in his favourite location beside the kitchen door. A few small calves, their heads stuck through the tubular bars of a gate are anxiously awaiting their turn to get into the yard for their evening meal. A haybarn, filled with hay, is situated opposite the house at the far side of the yard. Adjacent to the shed is the cowhouse. Four other small corrugated-roofed houses make up the composition of the farmyard.

The hum of a portable milking machine is heard. The owner of the property, Breda Kane and her friend, Nancy Clery, are milking the twelve cows. Apart from the small amount of money she is allocated from Brussels, Breda's main source of income is derived from the sale of milk, as well as the sale of the twelve calves the cows produce. She also rents out eleven acres of land to a well-off neighbouring farmer. A lot of her time is spent in her organic vegetable garden. In the main, she leads a frugal existence, helped by the fact that she is, to a large degree, self sufficient.

Having finished their work the two women go inside. Breda is forty one years old, Nancy is thirty nine. Both are mirror-images of each other in many ways, having dark hair, becoming speckled with grey now, inclined towards the plump side. Breda is the taller of the two. They are devoid of any facial make-up, wearing strong clothes suitable for outdoor work. They go down to the bathroom to wash their hands. 'The bit of help is great,' Breda comments.

'I'm afraid I wont be able to come over tomorrow evening.'

'That's okay,' Breda assures her. They make their way up to the kitchen. 'I intend to start and finish early anyway. Tomorrow night's the night.'

'I know,' Nancy replies. She goes and sits by the table, glancing down at an open newspaper. Breda busies herself getting out some delph. The kettle, whistling softly, is boiling away on the cooker. 'I only want a cup of tea.'

'Are you sure?'

'I had something when I got home from work – the usual. You're not having second thoughts then; you're going ahead with it?'

'I told you,' Breda replies. You think I'm mad, don't you?' Nancy's response of "No...no." doesn't carry much conviction. 'I can tell by your attitude.'

'It took me by surprise, that's all.' Head bent, she appears engrossed in the paper. 'Plenty of men here. Mad lookin' for women. What are they like though? That's what would worry me. I'd say there are some right quare hawks among 'em.'

'Nancy, I don't know. Look, what do you do? When you make your mind up you have to pick wan, don't you?' She stands behind Nancy, pointing with her finger. 'This is him, here.'

Nancy commences to read aloud. 'Lonely farmer in late forties, seeking a soulmate aged between thirty-five and fifty. Must enjoy country life and have a GSOH. Social drinker and occasional smoker.' She looks up. 'How is he "an occasional smoker?"'

'God, I don't know. Outside the door of the pub, maybe.'

'I wish I could control 'em like that.' She reads on. 'Considered handsome. Hobbies, G.A.A. and horse racing. Preferably replies from East Cork or West Waterford. Strictest confidence assured and expected.' She taps the paper with her finger. 'See that? He could be somebody we know.'
Breda crosses to the cooker, 'West Waterford and East Cork covers a big area. Anyway, it might be better if he didn't come from too far away. You'd be able to find out a few things about him.' She puts two spoons of tea in the teapot and pours in the hot water.

'Are you any little bit apprehensive about this?'

'Yeh, I am, a bit. But look Nancy, I've been looking around me, and I've been thinking. It's like this: I know there are girls going who don't need anyone. That's the truth. They're good looking, they're confident, they have good jobs, plenty of money and friends. They're happy the way they are. They don't need men in their lives. They have that choice. But look at me. The way I am.'

'How do you mean?'

'The way I am. I have no one.'

'That's not true.' Nancy looks aggrieved.

'I didn't mean it that way. I know I have you. But then, you're away in your job every day. You have your friends at work, people to talk to. I have no one most of the time. No company, apart from the old dog outside. Days I might only see the postman, or Billy Cahill, collecting the milk. Jesus, I sometimes feel I'm goin' out of my mind.'

'I know.'

'People say this is a grand spot to live in. It's not a very grand spot in the throes of winter. I've often stood there in the middle of that floor, gazing out the window at the wind and rain lashing across the fields, seeing the boughs bending down and slapping back again. Then you'd have to face out to do the jobs, with the rainwater running down the back of your neck. When you're on your own, the countryside can be a lonely tough place. That's wan thing you can be certain sure of.'

'I imagine,' Nancy concurs.

'The sheer loneliness of it – especially the nights.'

'I've been thinking about things myself, lately. You know, the people I work with aren't that close to me. They'd sicken you at times, to tell the truth. They keep on talking about their husbands, their boyfriends, their partners or whatever. They keep on an' on about it. All the lovely children they have; how brilliant and clever they all seem to be. I kinda feel left out of things. So you see, the town can be a lonely place too.... for some people.'

Breda pours out the tea. 'At least you have your folks to talk to in the evenings. Hear the day's gossip.'

'Gossip is right, small talk. Anyway, there's not much you can talk about with that man. He's a disaster.'

Breda indicates the paper again. 'See where he mentioned matches and horse racing; you know, I like the odd day out at the races now and then. They've been few and far between though'.

'Pity the way things turned out.' Nancy sympathizes. 'Christ, Breda, you got it hard, all those years.'

'Hard is right. But then, what can you do? You play the hand you're dealt. You have no option but to grin and bear it. You were great though, all along. I'll not forget it.'

'I wasn't,' Nancy says dismissively.

'Listen, I know nothing is going to come out of this thing now. I'll meet this fella and as sure as there's a sky above there'll be something wrong with him –or, more likely, he'll find something wrong with me.'

'Be careful, anyhow,' Nancy warns. 'The world is full of chancers – especially if they know you have property of your own. There are con-men out there looking for every opportunity.'

'That's what I want you for; you'll be able to size him up.'

'The two of us will.'

'Two heads are better than one. He mightn't even turn up yet. Still, he sounded genuine enough, to be honest. Sometimes you feel you can tell about a person.'

'That would be hard. The first time, over the phone?'

'He sounds a bit countryish. But then, look who's talkin'.'

Nancy's gaze reverts back to the paper. 'He says here he's considered handsome. Handsome! Imagine. He must be full of himself. If he's that "handsome" why is he still on the lookout in his late forties?—late fifties, more likely.' She smiles. 'He might have a head on him like that old puck goat above on the platform in Killorglin.'

'Looks like I'd better be prepared for all eventualities then.'

'Don't mind me. He might be really sound.' Sipping her tea, Nancy pores over the newspaper. 'You'd see some good ones here, wouldn't you? Look at this wan: "Gentleman of fifty-eight seeks mature lady for friendship and maybe more." What's the "maybe more" bit about?'

'A relationship, a friendship, I suppose.'

'Maybe something else,' she grins. 'Maybe he's a great oul' fella between the sheets. Years of experience at pleasuring women. Probably knows every trick in the book.'

'That's another thing: you know me, the kind of sheltered life I led, even before he got laid up?'

'Sheltered is the right word,' Nancy agrees.

'To tell the truth I have no experience of men.' Tentatively Breda continues. 'You know what I mean?.... that part of it.... you know' –she whispers—'the sex part of it? I don't know what I'd be like. Maybe I should tell him – level with him?'

'Do no such thing. Are you mad? Cracked! That's putting the cart before the horse. Do you want to run him straight away?'

'I might as well have been reared in a convent or something. Christ, I hope he's not some kind of pervert. You'd know anyway, wouldn't you?' Nancy shrugs her shoulders. 'Anyhow, I'm going ahead with it now, come hell or high water.'

'Why did you pick Tuesday night?'

'He said it's the quietest night of the week in the pub trade. There will be no one around, according to him. McTaggart's is the name of the place. Apparently there's a little lounge down a hallway. You get served through a hatch, like in the old days. "It's awful quiet at McTaggart's. We'll have the place to ourselves," he said.'

'Where exactly is it?'

'A couple of doors up from Doyle's shoe shop.'

'Oh yeh, I think I know it. It's a shook lookin' joint on the outside.'

'That's true alright,' Breda agrees. 'I drove in there for a look this morning. I walked up and down by it a few times. It seems dead quiet, like he said.'

'He can't live too far away then, seeing that he knows these places. Youghal is twelve miles in from here. He could be ten to fifteen miles on the other side — maybe more. Fellows like him are known to travel around a lot.'

'How do you mean – "fellows like him"?'

'He'd be movin' about a fair bit —on the lookout for women. I mean he'd have plenty of time on his hands, wouldn't he? I bet there'll be no flies on this guy. The old dog for the hard road.'

'I don't know. You make it sound as if I'm a right idiot.'

Nancy shakes her head. 'No, no, but you have to look at it every way. You have to prepare yourself in case he turns out to be a real arsehole.'

'I know,' Breda acknowledges in a resigned tone.

'But then, he mightn't,' Nancy continues. 'Like I said, don't mind me. Looking on the bright side, he might be a real genuine guy. Maybe he's a bit on the quiet side, lacking self-confidence. Could be lots of reasons why he's still a bachelor. Look at the way the years slipped by on us'

'That's true, when you think of it.' Breda suddenly clicks her fingers. 'God, I forgot; there's a piece of cake there in the —'

'No thanks,' Nancy quickly replies. Look at the belly I'm getting. I'll have to do something.'

'Same here.'

'I'm nearly eleven stone. Since it ended I'm gorgin' myself on sweet things. In my case I think it's called comfort eating.'

'Some of the things I have wont fit me anymore,' Breda comments.

'You're fine, honestly. Yeh, the years flew by alright. At least in your case you couldn't do much about it. Your hands were tied. But look at me? You know, I just can't get over it.'

'Nancy, don't be dwelling on that tramp.'

'Twelve years of my life going out with that fucker,' she

says with venom. 'Twelve years of my life –the best years, wasted. Dropped like a piece of dirt on the road. People coming up to me and saying how sorry they were. It was just awful! The humiliation, on top of everything else. Christ, when I didn't end up in the river I never will.'

'Like I told you, it might all be for the best. It just goes to show there's nothing in him. You'll see, he'll have no luck for it. He's tangled up with a right crowd now. I saw 'em the other day.'

'Did you?'

'She might be years younger than him but she looks a real bater.'

'I'd say so, she looks rough. I hope she kills him. I hope she breaks the fryin' pan over his fat, baldy, big fuckin' head. Anyway, it was that whole episode. Maybe that's why I'm so apprehensive about all men now.'

'Think of it as a lucky escape. He nailed his true colours to the mast, so you know you're missing nothing. If you stayed with him you could have put yourself in for a terrible life.'

'I don't know what to think. It's hard to get it out of your mind.'

'He's not worth thinking about, I'm telling you.'

Nancy rises, looking at her watch. 'Breda, you're very consoling. Anyway, it's not that but this. I have to head back. She's gone away again, so I have to get the ould fella's dinner. He'll be like a weasel if it's not ready on the table. This is the picture then: you're meeting him in the pub at eight o'clock tomorrow night. After a certain length of time I walk in – '

'Don't leave it too long.'

'We express surprise on seeing each other. Will he be dumb enough to buy that, I wonder?'

'What can he do about it? Make it sound convincing.'

'I only hope I can keep a straight face. You call me over and introduce me. I presume he'll offer to buy me a drink – even though he'd probably rather if a hole opened up and I fell through the floor. But he realizes he's stuck with me for a spell.'

'Between us we'll draw him out, see what he's like. You know, I've great confidence in you, Nancy.'

'God, don't say that. We can't be asking twenty questions; make it all too obvious.'

'No, we'll play it by ear. After awhile you'd get to know what a man is like, wouldn't you?'

'You're asking the right wan here! I wonder how is he going to react? He'll be tensed up too, you know. There he is, picture him now, bracing himself all day for the big occasion, and the next thing he's confronted by the two of us.'

'You're smart, you're good at making conversation, that's the thing. I'm no good.'

'You are,' Nancy tries to reassure her.

'I'm fine with you, I'd talk away all day. Sometimes I clam up when I meet people. Being on my own so much, maybe I've lost confidence in myself.'

'Whatever you do make an effort to talk to him anyway.'

'One to one I'm not too bad. In a crowd I'm useless. Listen, you'd hear reports about things like this working out sometimes, wouldn't you? Those "getting in touch" columns in magazines are fairly popular. Jesus, Nancy, where else can people like me meet someone nowadays?'

'There's the internet. That's the modern way of doing it, I believe.'

'What do I know about the internet – or computers.'

'I must show you some evening.'

'Will you?'

'It's not that difficult to get the hang of it. There's adult dancing as well, that's another way. Though I think it's mostly married people go to those places.'

'I'm not good at dancing either. God, I'm good at nothing.'

'Don't be like that.'

'I might have more in common with this fella. What I'm asking you to do is unusual, I know, but I'd love you to meet him, to see what you think. I've no one else to turn to.'

'After awhile I move off and leave you to it?'

'I suppose. Maybe I'd want to have my head examined, would I?'

'Another thing you'd want to do tomorrow is get some new clothes.'

'Next week. He can accept me or not the way I am.

I'm not going to put on any airs and graces for him.'

'What you have is a bit on the old-fashioned and dowdy side,' Nancy reminds her. 'But please yourself.' She crosses towards the door. 'See you tomorrow night then.'

'I'll see you off.'

They stroll out to where two small cars are parked in the front of the house. Nancy gets in, turns the ignition and the little Nissan Micra jumps into life. She noses the car out the narrow gateway and turns left. They wave to each other as Nancy drives carefully up the lane.

Chapter Two

Jimeen the Rat

Nancy's mind is in a whirl as she drives along. Breda's plan has her in a quandary: on the one hand she feels Breda is badly due a bit of good fortune and happiness; on the other hand she is aware of how much she would miss Breda if she started to date this man she intends meeting tomorrow night. Who knows, they might eventually even end up at the alter rails. 'The whole idea sounds preposterous! Breda of all people.' She shakes her head in disbelief. 'Breda never had any interest in men,' she muses. 'Then, I suppose she never got much opportunity.' She smiles to herself at the thought of Breda being actually intimate with some man. Didn't people say that if things were different at home Breda would probably have entered a convent. That would be unlikely, she thought, as she never found her over-religious or heard her talk much about the subject. Life is full of surprises and Breda definitely surprised her this evening. She would miss her because Breda was always dependable. If she wanted company to go someplace, Breda was there. She knew that some people found her a bit "different" for some reason.

She was quiet and reserved, maybe, and in the past didn't stir out much. People just didn't know her. The stark realization struck home that, apart from Breda, she had no one. 'Nobody!' The country is different to the town in that there aren't too many companions available. Certainly not in the townland of Redferne. People her age were either married, had emigrated, or were gone to work in the cities – especially Dublin. 'I'll leave this place,' she silently vowed. 'A dead-end job that I'm starting to hate.' She contemplated her situation. 'Where will I go though? That's the problem... I must do something.'

As she rounds a bend on the high road she becomes aware of the glorious sunset. The western sky presents a vast, crimson, beautiful panoramic vista. The swallows are diving, darting, weaving and chirping loudly, as they chase their prey. There was always a heavy laziness to those long, sultry, summer evenings. The wild flowers are in bloom and the hedgerows are awash with colour. Even the furze, which is not considered highly in the countryside, is now covered in a beguiling golden mantle. Nature is looking her best, but Nancy is not in the mood to appreciate her beauty. Images of her former lover, Fran Delaney, keep flashing into her mind. She has asked herself numerous times what happened, what did she do to him. It must have been something drastic, but she could think of nothing. On the contrary, didn't she do everything to please him: didn't she always try to pass herself well in company, tried to be witty and make good conversation. She remembered all the presents she bought him down the years. They were so intimate and close that the shock of being rejected was all the greater. A burning resentment towards this man is now building up, to replace the love she had harboured for him. 'He just used me,' she repeated, again and again, with venomous rancour.

She hadn't much time to dwell further, as the journey home was short and she was nearly there. The thought of her father waiting didn't improve her disposition. Jimmy Clery was the archetypal "street angel and house devil." Nancy was aware that he was widely known as

Jimeen the Rat. An episode when he was a young man was responsible for this most unflattering of titles: when he was twenty years old he went to where there was a public exhibition of the old-fashioned method of threshing corn. The event was run in conjunction with the local carnival, to raise funds for the hospital. A bench of oaten straw, saved in sheaves, had been erected. Men used pitchforks to toss the sheaves up onto the threshing mill; the corn was then fed into the machine and the grain collected in sacks underneath.

Jimeen, as he was then called, always wanted to be in the thick of things. He arrived along, grabbed a pitchfork and joined the other men in tossing the sheaves onto the threshing mill. The fun and banter at this type of event was usually of a high order. Beer was regularly distributed to quench the men's thirst. A rat suddenly leaped up from under the sheaf Jimeen was pitching; in its panic to escape it jumped into what it thought was a dark safe place – up the inside leg of Jimeen's trousers. If the rat was panicked it was nothing to the reaction of Jimeen: he roared and screamed and rolled around in his endeavours to extricate himself from this horror. The rat climbed up, reaching a very delicate and sensitive area of Jimeen's anatomy, where it bit and scratched as he frantically tried to crush and strangle it with his bare hands. Eventually he succeeded and the rat plonked down— its entrails hanging out— onto his shoe and onto the oats. There was a collective sense of shock and horror, but there was absolutely nothing anybody could have done. Ashen-faced, in a state of collapse, Jimeen was whisked away to the doctor. Before they continued, the rest of the men cut binder twine and fastened their trousers' above the ankles.

After about half an hour, when the initial shock wore off, some of the men started to giggle; after an hour most were guffawing loudly. Someone shouted "Jimeen the Rat!" There and then he was newly Christened. Ever since, if a local person bought a car for instance, and he was queried as to where he purchased it, the automatic reply invariably was "I got it from Jimeen the Rat," – or simply, "the Rat."

Jimeen had grown up to be a large, heavy man. He suspected well enough what he was called, and it was worse than a red rag to a bull. If anyone had the temerity to call him that to his face then that person stood a very good chance of being decapitated by a wheel brace.

Jimeen has two passions in life – playing golf and drinking pints of Guinness. He reckons he can do more business on the fairways and in the pubs that he does in the forecourt of the garage. For convenience sake his favourite watering hole is Black's pub, located near his own home. After a few drinks he usually takes centre stage, trotting off blue joke after blue joke. People often marvelled, as his repertoire seemed different on each occasion. If the fair sex were present Bobby Black had to tell him, "For God's sake Jimeen, keep it down, there are ladies present." Jimeen would make himself known to "the ladies." Despite his age he wasn't adverse to trying his luck with any female who caught his eye – be she married or single.

He tried hard to masquerade as a "hail-fellow-well-met" type of individual. Despite his best efforts he wasn't that well liked. People felt there was something superficial about him. They laughed at his jokes, but as soon as he left the premises they laughed at him as well.

"He's a quare fella," they said. As soon as he reached home the metamorphosis prevailed, and his family knew him as a contrary, cantankerous bully, possessing a very short fuse. Nancy's two sisters and a brother had long since departed, glad to escape their father's temper. Her mother had fled the house two days previously, the result of another row. Nancy knew from previous experience that she'd probably return home tomorrow, or the day after. She, herself, was able to stand up to her father much better than her mother. Didn't she take up a kitchen knife once and physically threaten to attack him. He got such a shock he quickly backed off. Ever since he treated Nancy with discretion, resentment and to a certain degree, grudging respect. She often wondered why her mother married him in the first place. They were as different as chalk and cheese. He, obviously, was loud and aggressive, whereas her mother was too quiet for her own good.

'He finishes around six, he'll surely call somewhere about a car, and then the pub, so he shouldn't be home yet,' she calculated. She was wrong; as soon as she turned in the gate she was confronted by his big four-wheel-drive, parked in front of the door. As she got out and locked the car she wondered what kind of humour she would find him in. He is sitting down, newspaper in hand, an angry scowl on his face.

'Where the feckin' hell were you?' he barks.

'Never mind,' Nancy replies.

'About time you got home. This is a nice state of affairs alright; a man comes home after a hard day and not a bloody morsel if food on the table.'

'It's a stew I have.' She busies herself putting the saucepan on the cooker and the cutlery on the table. 'It'll be ready in a few minutes. It's cooked already; all I have to do is re-heat it.'

'I'm starving, I'd ate a horse.'

'Are you home long?'

''Too feckin' long. Sittin' here like an idiot.'

'Why didn't you look around you. Surely you could have put the saucepan on the cooker? You're not that helpless.'

'The least a man could expect is to have his dinner on the table. That's not asking too much, is it?'

'I'm working too, you know,' Nancy reminds him.

'That other woman should be here. She's not worth a damn. At the drop of a hat she runs off to that sour-puss of a sister. And I'll tell you wan thing, if that bitch rings up again I'll give her Hopalong-Cassiddy.'

'If you kept your temper in check she'd be here.'

'You keep a civil tongue in your head. Where the hell were you, anyway? Oh, for feck sake, I need hardly ask – over with the quare wan, I suppose.'

'She's not a quare wan.'

'What else is she? Hidin' away like a bloody hermit. They were laughin' about her below in the pub the other night.'

'Why? Not that I mind what that bunch of ignoramuses say down there.'

'Jonny Moroney was down at her house fixin' some

electric gadget. She told him she heard the banshee wan night.' He smirks, 'The banshee, be Christ! The only banshee around here is your mother, with her long white hair.'

'No wonder it's grey – listening to you.'

'It wouldn't surprise me what you'd hear down at the end of that boreen. I believe that dog she have is vicious. Even the postman can't get out of the bloody van.'

'You'd need a good dog when you're on your own.'

'You're a feckin' idiot, wastin' your time with that wan. What the hell brings you down there, anyway? What do you be at?'

'Everything.' She fills and plugs in the electric kettle.

'She keeps cows. I didn't think you'd soil your delicate, manicured hands, with shitty-arsed cows.'

'You might be surprised then.'

'Nothing would surprise me with you.'

'I suppose they talk about everybody down in that friggin' pub? They should mind their own business,' Nancy says angrily. 'They think they're great, don't they? – laughin' at people. That's all they're good for. A crowd of bums!'

'The pub is the only place where I get a bit of pleasure. There's not much of it in this house.'

'You can say that again,' she responds. 'Look, the stew is nearly ready, the table is laid, the bread is cut, the kettle is boiling, so you can help yourself anytime you're ready.'

'Where are you off to now?'

'I'm going to my room. I have a few things to do.' She crosses.

'Hey, listen, I saw your old boyfriend today. He's lookin' well, really well,' Jimeen says with a cynical grin.

'Good!' She slams the door behind her and goes down the hallway and up to her bedroom.

Chapter Three

Redferne

Back at the farm, Breda decides she'll have a last look at the animals before retiring for the night. She is very much attached to all the livestock on the place. She has a name for each of the twelve cows and looks after the lot extremely well. Her favourite is one she calls Nosey. She was called this because if a door was left open, anywhere around the yard, Nosey would try to squeeze in. She gives her an apple as she passes by. Having satisfied herself that everything is alright Breda pauses, studying the yard, the shed, the few small out-houses and the dwelling house itself. She sighs a little as she looks about, resigning herself to the fact that a lot of improvements could be done to the place. 'If only I had the money.' Money was never really a factor with her. All she ever wanted was enough money to get by, to pay her debts promptly. Her faithful dog, Glen, is sitting at her feet, looking up into her face. He doesn't look like a dog who is the terror of all postmen. She pats his head a few times. She decides that tomorrow she'll give the yard a thorough cleaning. She recalls when she was performing this task back in April. In fact, the memory remains vividly etched in her mind:-

Breda's sister, Betty, wrote to say that herself, her husband Dave, and her two young daughters were coming to Ireland on vacation. Dave always wanted to visit Ireland, and they had booked into an hotel in Killarney. The letter stated that they'd be arriving at Shannon on Friday the fifteenth, and that they intended calling to the farm the following Tuesday. Betty had also telephoned to confirm this. Breda remembers being very excited over the news. In all the years, Betty had been home only once, briefly, for the funeral. Now she was visiting with her husband and two little girls, Lily and Jenny. She remembers being a little bit apprehensive as well. She wondered what would Dave and the girls think of the place. She had resolved to spend all day on Monday cleaning up the yard. She was engrossed in this task, pushing a wheel-barrow of farmyard manure across the yard, when who should arrive along but her American visitors – a day early. The big car swung in the gateway, and she hadn't a chance to run, to wash and change her clothes. (Big cars and other large vehicles used the yard to turn, as the space in front of the house was too narrow) Red-faced she greeted everyone, after first wiping her hands on her overalls. 'Oh God!' she now says, flinching, putting her hand up to her face, again feeling the embarrassment. Straight away, Dave had struck her as being a very nice individual. He stood there smiling, a happy, boyish looking, tanned American. He gave her a kiss on the cheek and a hug. Betty hugged her close as well. Betty looked great, laden down with jewellery, as slim as ever. She was the youngest of the three girls, the most popular and attractive member of the family. Without it being the least intentional Betty, for some reason, always made Breda feel inadequate. They had hired out a car and decided to tour the country a day early. Betty said she had phoned a few times but there was no answer. Breda silently remembers cursing her stupidity in forgetting to give her mobile number.

Breda was acutely aware that the two young girls were unimpressed either by herself or the appearance of the place. They had looked at her with a sullen expression, refusing any body contact. In fact, they cowed away from her as if she were some kind of ogre. Breda couldn't wait to get in, to quickly wash, change her clothes and tidy herself. The bathroom door was ajar and she heard Lily say "She's gross." Jenny said, "The whole place is gross." Their parents reprimanded them crossly. Betty said, "For God's sake, behave yourselves." Lily piped up, "Mummy, sure we're not going to eat here?" Jenny added, "The place is smelly and dirty." Then, when Breda returned to the kitchen, Dave said, "Breda, we're sorry for crashing in on you like this. You mustn't put yourself to any bother over us. What we'll all do is go into that little town—Dungarvan, isn't it? –and have a nice lunch in the hotel." Breda remembers apologizing, saying that if she knew they were coming she'd have had the dinner ready. After a pleasant meal in the hotel they had returned to the farm. Dave commented on how beautiful the scenery was; how it was true about everyplace being so green. How he couldn't wait to travel round this fascinating country. He was happily snapping away with his new digital camera. He explained the workings of this new technology to Breda. The two girls fell in love with the calves. Glen was suspicious at first, but then allowed himself to be patted. He followed Dave, Lily and Jenny, when they went off through the fields to see the lake. Breda remembers being glad, to be finally alone with Betty. Concerned, Betty said she thought Breda looked tired, and drawn. She suggested that maybe Breda was working too hard. "Take it easy," she said. All this now flooded back into Breda's mind. The way Betty quizzed her about all the people they knew. "How was so-an-so getting on? Did she ever marry?" She commented that Ireland was an expensive place to live nowadays. "Things are cheaper in Chicago." Dave was earning big money, and the girls were doing well at school. Breda said what a nice man Dave was, and the two girls were very pretty. "Very bold at times, too. It's just that they're not in the habit of anything a bit on the yucky side – like a farmyard." Breda said she understood.

The time had passed rapidly and the visitors were about to depart. Dave and Betty hugged her again. Dave said they had a marvellous time. After being well tutored Lily and Jenny said, "Goodbye, Aunt Breda." The way Betty— before she climbed in to the car— had thrust three one-hundred euro notes into Breda's hand. Breda recalls standing at the gate, watching the car edge up the lane. Hands waved out the windows and she waved back. As the car disappeared she had felt a tinge of sadness. How long would it be before she saw them all again? She had also experienced some relief as, by and large, things hadn't gone that bad – apart from the attitude of the children, which stung a little. They had caught her at her worst and she wondered what Dave really thought. When the car had faded from view, she remembers looking down at the notes in her hand and feeling a tear run down her cheek. She went back inside to change; the presents were still there on the table – the box of biscuits, the flowers, the large box of Black Magic.

The memories are still sharply in front of her now, as she crosses to go indoors for the night. 'Betty is such a lucky person,' she acknowledges to herself. 'She doesn't know what it's like to be lonely. She has a fine husband and family.' She sighs. 'I wonder what will my fellow be like, tomorrow night. God, I hope he'll be alright.'

Chapter Four

On a Similar Track

Around about the same time Ned Power is approaching his farmhouse, returning from the high field where he has checked on the cattle before darkness sets in. He has on his worn working clothes, has strong boots on his feet and a cap on his head. He is unshaven, of medium build, of wiry stature. Ned is fifty years of age but looks a few years more. There is a run-down, neglected appearance to the farm buildings, and to the dwelling house itself. None has seen any paint for a considerable number of years. The farm is situated on high ground and is often referred to as "The Hill Farm."

Ned pauses at the gateway to the yard, looks around, passes wind loudly and urinates against the gatepost. He coughs long and hard a few times the result, no doubt, from years of heavy smoking. He mumbles, 'Them feckin' fags are killin' me!' The Power name has survived in this farm for generations. Numerous hardships were overcome down the years. Helped by the produce of the farm, Ned's ancestors even survived the Great Famine. Traditionally the eldest son inherited the farm, whilst the rest of the family emigrated. America was usually the favoured destination. The ones who went rarely returned. The night before the sad journey to the quayside, an event was held in the house called an "American Wake." The neighbours and friends gathered to bid farewell, and usually a lot of alcohol was consumed to deaden the heartache. Ned was aware that he was probably the last in the family line. This was a realization he didn't like to dwell on. He often imagined himself married to Joan Kiely. Wondered what it would be like to hear the laughter of children, as they romped about the farmstead. He remembered how he was stone mad about Joan. He was still haunted by her sunny personality and her big warm smile. He despaired at the fact that she refused to marry him. The memory of that night remained ingrained in his mind. He loved her and could think of no one else. It took him a long time to get over the disappointment. His mother was hale-an-hearty back then, and she didn't take too kindly to the thought of another woman moving into the house. She made this plain to Joan, on the one and only occasion he brought her home. That was probably the big stumbling block to their romance. He had no money to build his own house. It just wasn't the done thing, back in those days. 'Two cooks in the one small kitchen could cause a problem alright,' he surmised. At that period, even though he was in his mid-thirties, his mother still referred to him as "the young boy." If the truth be known, his mother didn't want to lose her "young boy" to a strange woman from Youghal. Yes, without a doubt, Joan Kiely was the love of his life. 'Everybody has wan,' he concludes. 'The lucky wans stay together for the remainder of their days. That's the way life is, I suppose,' he laments. Lately he was getting into the habit of speaking out loud his innermost thoughts. He resolved to stop this silly practice.

If he hits it off with this woman tomorrow night there are a few things he'd want to change: he'd want to cut back on the booze for a start – especially on the nights he'd be meeting her. 'Christ, what would I do if I got nabbed by the cops and me license went! I'd be in right cloud cuckoo-land then.' He tried to conceal the fact from himself that he had a bit of a problem with the booze. Nothing to worry about. It was just that he found it hard to stop after a couple; it just put him in the mood for a few more. He paused, as he assessed himself. 'Ah feck it, I'm not too bad. I'm not as hard on it as Nicky. I can carry it too, better than him.' He walked slowly across the yard, towards the back kitchen door. 'It would take a lot now to put me on me back. I'm conditioned to the stuff...

I wonder what will she be like at all?' he asks himself for the umpteenth time. He is feeling slightly apprehensive now, as the time is fast approaching. He reaches down under a stone but the key is missing. He knows straight away that Nicky has arrived. He crosses over, and as the door is unlocked proceeds in. Sure enough, Nicky is sitting there, reading a newspaper he has spread out on the table in front of him. The kitchen left a lot to be desired as regards tidiness and cleanliness; things are scattered about in a haphazard fashion, unwashed cups and saucers clutter the sink; a strip of wallpaper is hanging loose on the back wall; turf, and a few logs are smouldering in the open fire.

Nicky Daly is a year younger than Ned. He is dressed in a somewhat similar fashion – hard wearing old clothes, boots, sporting a felt hat with a feather to the side. The two men are similar in lots of ways: Nicky is also a bachelor, who depends for his livelihood on another small hilly farm close by. Nicky's two elderly parents live with him in the farmhouse. This arrangement, down the years, also curtailed his chances of finding a wife. His circumstances were always no better than Ned's, so his prospects of building a second home were also out of the equation. Nicky's fascination with the opposite sex is still very apparent. He hasn't given up hope yet of locating a partner, to take home to his little farm on the hillside. His chances, however, are diminishing by the year. The two men are not unlike numerous other bachelors spread throughout the rural landscape of Ireland.

Ned and Nicky are close friends, who practically go everywhere together. This friendship developed, despite the fact that in the old days their families were bitterly divided over politics. Ned's family were strong supporters of Fine Gael, whereas Nicky's were staunch Fianna Fail devotees. This affiliation in the political spectrum was responsible for someone calling Ned "Mick Collins" and Nicky "The Long Fella." They were still called this, in jest, in Black's pub, two titles that irritated them intensely. They had disowned politics years ago, they reminded their audience.

Nicky looks up as Ned enters. 'Everything all right?' he inquires.

'Yeh, yeh, everything's fine,' Ned replies.

'How are the cattle lookin'?'

'Lookin' well. Good growth in the grass. You can't bate the bit of sun. The weather is settled, I'd say.'

'I wouldn't bet on it. You're thinkin' of sellin' at the right time. Prices are up, I hear.'

'Ah, I don't know. Hard to tell with prices. Up wan day, down the next. Up and down like a whore's knickers.'

Nicky smiles at the comparison. 'You have knickers on your mind the whole time.'

'Not as much as you.'

'I wonder what colour will this wan be wearin' tomorrow night?'

'I must ask her to show you.' Ned has another bout of coughing and he spits phlegm into the coal-scuttle. 'Them effin fags will be the death of me. I must give 'em up. No two ways about it.'

'They're hard bastards to kick. I was just lookin' at your ad. here on the paper. I read it at home already. You know, it's well put together. You done a fair good job with it.'

Ned looks pleased. 'I copied bits out of other wans.' He points to the paper. 'It mightn't be entirely accurate – me age, an' that – but if you're goin' to tell a lie you might as well err on the side of discretion.'

'No use frightening them off at the startin' gate,' Nicky agrees. 'You might have put down that you're a man of substance, sound in wind and limb.'

Ned crosses to the sideboard. 'Nicky, we're not dalin' with a horse here. This might have a damn serious ending yet. Me whole life could change over them few lines. See where I put down, "Replies from East Cork and West Waterford." I find the women from around the Dungarvan side have a good ould sense of humour. And jasus boy, that's an important asset in a woman. No use lookin' across the table at a face that would stop a clock, for the rest of your natural days.'

'True, true. A sound country girl, with a big smile on her face that would brighten up your day. Someone like Joan Kiely.'

'Exactly.' Ned returns to the table with a bottle of Paddy whiskey. 'Yeh, Joan had that personality alright. It's all water under the bridge now, boy. I slipped up there, slipped up in a big way. Damn near broke me heart, and that's the truth. I still think of her. When you get older and look back, the more precious them times appear. You know it's never goin' to happen to you again. It's Paradise lost boy, gone for ever.'

'Sure we had nothing back in those days,' Nicky states. 'We hadn't two pennies to rub together. Maybe she knew that. She didn't want a life of poverty.'

'We had nothing is right. "The good old days," how are yah! There was nothing bloody good about 'em. Nothing bloody good that I can remember, anyhow. You had to slave day and night to make a few pounds. The cupboard was often bare. We were like the tinker's dog, boy – we saw more dinner times than dinners.'

Nicky's eyes are still down, studying the paper. 'Why the hell did you put down, "considered good looking?" Now she'll be expecting something better than you to walk in the door.'

'When I'm tidied I'm not the worst.' He rubs his chin. 'Shaved an' that. I thought it best to look for replies close enough to home. That way, a woman would kind of understand our way of doing things.' He pours a good measure of whiskey into the two glasses and goes to locate a water jug. 'Know what I mean?'

'Safer maybe than spreading the net too wide. Christ, I keep thinkin' of Jonny McNulty.'

'He went far enough anyway – Thailand, be God.' He

pours water into the whiskey.

Nicky quickly raises an arm. 'Enough! Don't drown it. But by God she's a fair looker. Like I said before, nothin' to touch her in this parish.'

'Or the next. She's what you'd call a jewel of a woman, an emerald, a sapphire.'

Nicky says, 'Good-luck.' Ned responds likewise. Nicky sips the whiskey and pokes Ned with his elbow. 'Hey, Ned, how would you like to have her legs wrapped around you above in the bed?' They both laugh.

'I'd manage her boy, I'd manage her.'

'No better man. Would the old heart stick it? Tell me this though: how the hell did he get her? That's what I can't understand. What is it she sees in him?' Nicky is perplexed. 'There's the huge age gap. I can't figure it out. It's a strange business.'

'And she seems mad about him. She hangs out of him.' Ned goes across and stokes up the fire with a poker. Sparks rise up. 'Fair play to him. He had the courage to go out there. He don't give a damn what people think either. I envy the man. I'm not ashamed to say it.'

'We all envy him,' Nicky agrees with fervour. 'What I wouldn't give for wan like that. Notice the legs; the way she walks; the way she swings the hips – like a well oiled machine.' Nicky attempts to demonstrate, but stops abruptly. 'You know, me own joints aren't the best right now. I have a dead leg, or something.' He flicks his leg out a couple of times, starts to vigorously massage the calf with both hands, and stamps the foot on the floor.'

'Is it hurting you?'

'No, it's just kinda stiff. I have to get the circulation goin'. It'll be alright.'

'Would you want to go about it?'

'No, I'll wait an' see how it goes. Go on, anyhow? What were you sayin'?'

'Nothin'…. You know something, them youngwans from around here wouldn't be long about giving you a dose of reality.'

'How do you mean?' Nicky inquires, his leg seemingly back to normal.

'The old music started below in the pub not so long ago. You weren't there. Anyway, I went across and asked a couple of young girls out to dance. They only laughed at me. Laughed up in my face. That's the truth. Had to turn around and walk back. And I'll tell you wan thing boy, you'd feel a right fool walkin' back across the floor with your tail between your legs. Seeing O'Connor's big mouth, laughin' at you.'

'Feck him! Scoffin' an' laughin' is all that bastard's good for. Dancing, you said! What them young people do is not dancin'. Standing there shakin' their arses and waving their arms in the air.' Nicky gives a comical imitation of same.

'Later on, when I came home, I went and stood in front of that mirror for a good while; looking at that craggy, lined, weather-beaten ould face. And I said to myself, "Cop yourself on Power, you ignorant, stupid, thick fool. Them young girls want no truck with someone who reminds them of their own father."'

'That's cracked talk. What about McNulty then?'

'Forget about McNulty. You know something, that woman will have you driven demented. She's on your mind the whole time. The next thing you'll be doin' is headin' off for Bangkok.'

'I'm just saying, there he is; no trouble to him. She's half his age, I'd say – maybe not even that.'

'There's McNulty and there's us. Anyway, I said to myself again, "Power, it's about time you faced up to reality – faced up to the harsh truth: the years have caught up with you. Your race is run, your race is run."'

Nicky is not impressed. 'Bullshit! It's all in the mind – up here in the head. It's just the way you're feelin' tonight. It's the man's personality the women go for, not his age.'

Ned is adamant. 'Your race is run too, Daly, me friend. You might as well admit it. You're fecked, the same as myself.'

'I'm not fecked. Far from it. That's throwin' in the towel.'

Ned continues along the same line. 'The two of us are out on grass. We're on the scrap-heap.'

'That's stupid talk. You know what that is – that's codology you're talkin'. Feckin' codology. I don't believe it for a minute. I know plenty of men who are years older than their wives; years and years older. If you have the money you'll get the woman.'

'Maybe, with a lot of money, a huge amount of money. But what have we got?'

'The age difference was always there. Look at all the widows that are around. Plenty of 'em. Not too many widowers though.' He winks the eye and shakes the head. 'Notice that?'

'You think it's two young widows we should be scoutin' for, then?' Ned asks.

'Maybe. Why not? If you throw the hands up in the air you're bet, you're bet. Jasus, remember all the good times we had, travelling around. How many miles did you say is clocked up in that Bluebird outside? – over two hundred thousand. How many times did we hit Kerry, Galway? – all over the place. What about Lisdoonvarna? Drinkin' an' dancin', day and night, for a week.'

'Where did it get us in the end? Look at us. We thought it would never end. We kept goin' too long.' With a quick motion he removes Nicky's hat, as well as taking off his own cap. 'Look at us; we hardly have enough hair left between us to line a bird's nest.'

Nicky snatches back his hat. 'Gimme that.'

Ned replaces his own cap. 'Like I was saying, you have to take stock of the situation. I'm almost fifty-wan boy, and you're not lagging far behind. Do you remember all the fellows we grew up with? In the national school?'

'Sure I do. A lot of 'em are scattered now. Most of 'em I'd say.'

'Scattered is right,' Ned emphasises. He crosses and

stands, gazing out the window. 'A few of them are dead; a good few more went to England – and a couple of those were never heard of again. America, Canada and Australia took a share.'

'That's the way, that's life.'

Ned returns centre again. 'Then you have the wans who stayed around here and have families. Things went well for 'em and they're happy and contented with life. They have a good future ahead of them to look forward to. But what have we to look forward to? That's the thing you see, that's the thing.'

Nicky doesn't care to hear this. 'Hold on a minute now, hold your horses. 'Tisn't all married bliss either. Be jasus, no. I could name several who are fightin' like cats an' dogs. Better single any day than livin' that kind of life.'

'Some are split up too. I know, I know all that. Okay, the answer is to be careful. Be damn careful who you pick.'

'Is putting an ad. on the paper the right way to go then?'

Ned pours more whiskey into the glasses. 'The advantage in being a bit long in the tooth like us is that surely we should be able to size a person up. We're hardly that stupid.'

'The old dog for the hard road bit again?'

'Exactly. All that remains then is to see what way the cat jumps tomorrow night. I have a feelin' in me bones she's goin' to be no film-star. Otherwise she'd have been snapped up ages ago. Wouldn't she? What do you think?'

Nicky scratches his chin philosophically. 'You never know. She could have a reason. Lots of reasons.'

Ned taps the paper with his finger. 'Thirty-five to fifty I put down here; when she arrives she'll probably be nearer the sixty mark. To hell with it! No one will see us inside at Jimmy McTaggart's.'

'She might have a face on her down to here,' Nicky adds, 'and a pair of legs on her like two milk churns. But then again, you never know. She might surprise you.'

'To be honest, she sounded a decent, honest-to-God, down-to-earth kind of person. If she's half right at all I'll give her another chance. Nicky boy, all I want now is a good companion, a friend, someone to share life's joys and sorrows with. Someone to come home to, who'll have a smile on her face and a bite of hot food on the table. She don't have to be Miss Thailand.'

'Ah-hah,! Nicky exclaims triumphantly. 'There you are! Thinkin' about her too. You're some old hypocrite!'

'I'm thinkin' about tomorrow night. Look at the old Bluebird outside: she's starting to rattle an' groan an' creak now. Age is catchin' with her. It's goin' to be the same with us from now on.'

'There you go again. It's a pity they didn't dance with you. It's them youngones have you the way you are.'

Ned dreams wistfully. 'How would you like it if you were married now, and the wife said to you: "So you have a pain between the shoulders Nicky boy. Lie down there now and take off the shirt and vest and I'll get the poteen and rub it in." 'Or,' "Nicky, I don't want you going out in the rain and getting wet, in case the old arthritis kicks in. The old hips might come against you. Sit down there now by the fire and warm yourself, and I'll get you a good drop of hot whiskey.'"

Nicky stares at him in disbelief. 'Are you feelin' right in the head this evenin'? Are you goin' cracked or something? Jasus boy, cop yourself on. Marriage is a deadly dangerous business nowadays. Those new Family Protection Laws are a minefield. I'm tellin' you now; they can trip a man up in a big way.'

'You know all about 'em, I suppose?'

'I know enough about 'em. You get married and, according to the laws of the land, the wife, straight away, will own half of everything you have. The other day, after the funeral, a couple of us were talking to Billy Joyce. Everywan knows Joyce is a smart man. Marriage came up. "I'm never getting married," he said. "You walk up to the alter with your whole farm, but when the priest is done with you, you'll turn around and walk back down the aisle with half a farm."'

'Ned's features register surprise. 'He said that?'

'Damn sure he did,' Nicky says with authority. 'If the marriage didn't work out, where would you be then, huh?' Be jasus, 'tisn't rubbin' in the poteen you'd be.'

'You'd be afraid to chance it, would you?'

'I'd think twice. What good would half a farm be to us?'

'You're right there; no good, no good at all.'

'They're small enough as it is,' Nicky confirms.

Glass in hand, Ned crosses over to the window again. 'The thing is, you see, you have to get to know the person really well. You have to trust a person. Marriage, I'd say, is all about trust. Don't rush things, give yourself plenty of time. Maybe tomorrow night I'll have a fair idea.' He suddenly turns around, blurting out, 'Christ, I wont! You know me. I'm no good at these things! I'm feelin' kinda quare about it already. Maybe I'm puttin' my foot in it. You come in now, not too long after meself.'

Christ, I don't know. Like I said, two's company.'

'Three is better company.'

'It'll look odd. She'll know we planned it.'

'It's a public house, isn't it? Look, do this for me. I don't often ask you. Now, you just ramble in, as if it's the most natural thing in the world. We'll act a little surprised to see each other. You know, make it look good. Ah sure, you'll know well what to say – aren't you always tellin' lies.'

'Only you think that! I'm not too happy about this. Anyway, you're meetin' her at eight o'clock, you said?'

'What'll I say to her at all? How'll I break the ice?'

'You were always a good talker with the women.'

'Don't be coddin' me. You're the one who was always glib on the tongue. It'll be a lot handier now, with the three of us there. You'll be able to put her at her ease, know what I mean? Then, when we're all relaxed an' talking away, you can finish up your drink and shag off to hell out of the place.'

'Wan piece of advice I'll give you: don't have too many whiskies inside you when you meet her. You can be a right idiot when you drink too much whiskey.'

'We can all be idiots when we drink too much whiskey.'

'You look stupid and you talk rubbish.'

'You can be as contrary as hell too.'

'Can I now! You should hear yourself though.'

'I'll only have a few to steady me down.'

'Listen, if things go well with you now, and you start meeting this girl more often, you'll have to ask her along here.' He glances about. 'She wouldn't be too impressed with the cut of this place, I'll tell you that for nothing. You'll have to go over it from head to toe.'

'I know, I know.'

'Modern women expect every luxury; a second television for the bedroom, I imagine.'

'Tisn't watchin' television I'll be boy. Anyway, the bit of comfort wouldn't go astray.'

Nicky stands by the sink. 'A washing machine for this china here.' Using two fingers he gingerly holds up an unwashed plate.. 'Look at this. You wouldn't want her getting food poisoning with a bad dose of diarrhoea on her first visit. There's a whole load of things you'll have to think about. It's not goin' to be all plain sailin', not by a long shot.'

'Don't be puttin' obstacles in my way. I'll cross all those bridges when I get to 'em.'

'You'd want to cross 'em quick. You know something, she'd get an awful fright if she done a grand tour of this house. Christ, you could spend a fortune on it.'

'We'll have to wait an' see what happens first, wont we?' Ned says, slightly irritated.

'I hope I'm wrong now, but be careful. Be fierce careful. She might be wan of those women who'll break you out. She mightn't give a tinker's curse what the farm itself is like, providin' the house is like a palace. Before long, there might be nothin' grazing them fields out there only snipe and curlews.'

'Will you shut up be damned. She's from a farm. She understands things.'

Nicky is unconvinced, 'Makes no difference. I hear stories about what can happen.'

'You hear stories about everything,' Ned responds. 'Maybe that's why there are so many like us around. Always afraid, always thinkin' the worst, always suspicious of everything. You mind yourself now, what you're goin' to say to her.'

'What do you mean, like?'

'Don't say anything that might paint me in a bad light. You know what I'm getting at? Say complimentary things.' He places an arm on Nicky's shoulder. 'I'm depending on you now, for me to create a good impression.'

Nicky is taken aback. 'Depending on me! That's a good wan. You're depending on me!'

'Ned pacifies him. 'Ah, shut your mouth. Here have a fag. And make sure you're in good form tomorrow night.' Each takes a cigarette from the box Ned holds out.

'Talk about puttin' a gun to a man's head. Anyway, what about tonight then?' Nicky queries. 'Are you goin' down to Black's?'

'Maybe 'twould be a bit dodgy, huh? That squad car travels the by-roads now, as well. All them accidents. What do you think?'

'I dunno.' Nicky is a little hesitant. 'Wouldn't want you to get caught.'

'Haven't we the bottle there,' Indicating the bottle of whiskey. 'There's a few cans of beer around there somewhere. Will that suit you?'

'Yeh, that'll do. Nothin' much happens down there on a Monday night anyhow.'

Ned cracks a match and they light up their cigarettes. Even though it's a warm night the traditional turf fire is smouldering away in the grate. They pull two chairs up and settle down. There is a silence as they draw on their cigarettes and sip the whiskey, feeling secure, relaxed and contented with each other's company.

Chapter Five

Foxy and Trish

The following evening, Foxy arrives home from work to his two-bedroom dwelling, on the outskirts of Youghal. He parks his eight year old Corolla beside the footpath and hops out. He shares the house with his partner, Trish. He is thirty years old, of slim build, muscular and fit. His hair is spiked and silver rings adorn his eyebrows and ears. The cement dust that clings to his shoes and clothes suggests correctly that he works in the building trade.

He keeps three well fed dogs in a enclosed yard, adjacent to the bedroom window. The dogs excitedly bark their greeting when they see him arrive. Leaning over the wall he addresses them: 'You're three great dogs, aren't you.' Reaching down he rubs their heads. The dogs respond by jumping up and down, tails wagging furiously. Going inside he greets Trish gaily. 'Christ, 'tis some evening.'

'It's terrific altogether,' she responds. 'It's nearly too hot. You'd sweat like a pig. There's supposed to be a change on the way though.'

'Hope not. Had you a hard day?'

'Tough enough. The usual. And you?'

'A real feckin hard day. We had to finish off a job. That's why I'm back a bit early. Anyway, it keeps you fit.' Smiling, he bends his arm, the muscles becoming apparent. 'Feel that.'

Trish is a striking, buxom looking young woman, well endowed in all areas. As the evening is so warm and sultry she is scantily clad. Foxy points to the cooker. 'My nose tells me there's something good in there.'
'It's just a fry. I hadn't much time.'
'The mobile is handy, isn't it?'
'Yeh, handy that way.'
'I'll give the paws a rinse.' He hurries down to the bathroom. Trish takes a plate of food out of the cooker – French-fries, burgers and beans – and places it on the table.
'Just what I like,' he says, coming back up and looking down at the table. He tucks into the food with relish, in tandem with a bottle of beer he has uncorked. Having eaten already, Trish makes do with a cup of tea and a scone.
'You're looking well this evening, really well,' he grins mischievously. 'You look real sexy.'
'She smiles a satisfied smile, saying, 'I don't know about that.'
'Did you get a chance to walk the dogs?' he asks.
'Yeh, around wan o'clock. A good walk too.'
'I'll take 'em out again. 'Twas fairly windy where we were today. All that friggin' dust. I was spittin' up black stuff all day. Could do with a breath of fresh air in me lungs.'
'I fed 'em before you came in.'
'Good. They're okay then.' There is a strong mutual affection between dogs and man. 'I saw Nicky Daly from Glentallagh, drivin' into town.'

'Oh did you. Nicky! Didn't see him around for a good while.'

'Black's pub is their usual haunt. Christ, you should see the cut of the car – covered in mud; never saw the bate of it. He must drive it around the fields. I missed him when I was out that way on Sunday. He was on his own in the car. I'd bet you a pound to a penny though, Ned is around somewhere.'

'They're always together, aren't they? The company, I suppose. 'Tis a lonely oul' place, out there.'

'Some scenery though. We'll have a bit of a craic if we bump into 'em.'

'We're hardly goin' out again tonight?'

'We'll see.'

Finishing the meal, he goes down for a shower. Trish cleans the table and washes up. The kitchen is spotless, neat and tidy, something she prides herself on. Foxy soon comes back – in the nude. Since the hot weather had arrived, both of them, periodically, had taken to walking about the house naked.

'I'm goin' to stretch out for a few minutes and have a smoke,' he says. 'Like to join me? Come on.'

'Okay,' she nods. 'In a minute.'

He goes up and slumps down on the bed. Having finished tidying the kitchen, Trish joins him. Foxy has rolled two joints. They lay back, light up, inhale deeply, exhale slowly, watch the smoke waft up to the ceiling.

''The cops done me this evening,' he announces.

Alert, she straightens up. 'What! What for?'

'Bald tyres.'

'Fuck 'em!'

'Fuck 'em is right. I don't mind that. A few quid. It's the drink they're tryin' to get me on.'

'Did they breathalyse you?'

'No, they knew I was dry.'

Trish is annoyed now. 'More money. Why hadn't you everything right? Christ, I told you not to give 'em the chance. Don't you know you can't bate 'em? They'll always get you in the long run. I told you that. Why don't you just listen to me sometime? Why are you such a feckin' idiot?'

Foxy is unperturbed. 'Come on, don't be like that. Come here to me.'

'Go way from me.' She pushes his hand away. 'Do you hear me? I want to finish this.' He persists, reaching across again. 'No, go away!'

'A lovely sexy girl like you shouldn't be getting annoyed over nothing.'

'Over nothing!' He tickles her under the armpits. She commences to giggle. She screams, 'No! Stop! Stop!' She hysterically kicks her legs in the air, and laughs in uncontrollable bursts.

As the window is open the dogs are getting a little disconcerted with this loud noise. They sit up on their bums, cock their ears, and look towards the bedroom window. Bruce, the biggest and cleverest of the three goes over and heaves his front paws up onto the window ledge; straining his back legs, and craning his neck, he does his best to see inside. Bruce has made a mistake: as he endeavours to focus his vision to the somewhat darkened interior, a soft Wellington boot zooms across and hits him straight between the eyes, knocking him back on the hard concrete. Loud laughter now emanates from inside.

Chapter Six

The Rendezvous

Nicky has arrived in Youghal early. Seeing that he has to go in to town in any case, to accommodate Ned, he decides to incorporate a bit of shopping. His main purpose is to call to the chemist, to acquire something for his troublesome leg. Then he has his magazines to collect. He also decided to invest in a comfortable pair of shoes. 'That should be a big help,' he reasoned.

Before he left home he had prepared a meal his elderly parents would have, later on, for their supper. This consisted of cooked ham, tomatoes, lettuce and beetroot. Nicky's father and mother – Paddy and Mary – were both in their late seventies. He always tried to look after the old folk as best he could. People commented on this, saying, "For a man who's a martyr to the drink, he couldn't be faulted on that account."

He now guides his car down the little street close to the water's edge, where Ned and himself always parked. The reason for this is twofold: firstly the parking is free, secondly it means avoiding the heavier traffic around the town centre. 'I never saw it as quiet as this,' he muses to himself, 'no car here but me own.' He looks at his watch and realizes he'd better get a move-on before the shops close. The chemist sells him an elastic stocking, but advises him that he'd really want to see a doctor. 'More money down the drain,' he sighs, as he goes out the door. The next port of call is Mackey's shoe shop. Twenty minutes later after much bickering over price –five euro deducted – a purchase is made. Now the little bookshop on the corner. The owner, a Mister Leech, reaches down behind the counter and hands Nicky a brown paper wrapped parcel of soft-porn magazines. Nicky pays up and hurries out the door, very few words having been spoken, or very little eye contact having being made. A kind of mutual conspiracy. Mister Leech smiles at the girl assistant behind the counter, nodding his head at Nicky's departing figure. She smiles back knowingly. Nicky reads those magazines avidly, and keeps them hidden under the mattress of his bed. He has an acute curiosity about all things appertaining to the opposite sex. He heard 'em say in the pub that if you bought a video recorder or a DVD player, you could rent out material and see the real thing. This whetted his appetite to an insatiable degree. 'How could he get his hands on wan of them?' he wondered, 'without the people knowing.' Maybe they were only pulling his leg. They were always teasing and goading Ned and himself. 'That basterin' O'Connor with his, "Did you get any bit lately, Nicky?" 'That man will go too far wan of these days, and I'll pull on him,' he promised himself. 'Then the Weasel Walsh, with his dirty, black-toothed grin,' "Jasus Nicky, them foreign women are great. No bother at all, boy. For fifty euro you'd get it any night of the week at the back of Dunne's Stores." "Take my advice and don't go near 'em," the sensible and decent Bobby Hartley said. "You wouldn't know what you'd pick up off them. You might rue the day you parted with your fifty euro." Ned or himself never did go near those women they spoke and laughed about. They probably didn't exist, in any case. As far as he could see those foreign girls looked decent and respectable. 'Fine lookin' girls too,' he generalized, as a couple walked towards him.

'What's Ned's woman goin' to be like at all?' he wonders, smiling at the thought of what lies ahead. 'We'll have a session anyway, no matter what happens,' he assures himself. Glancing at his watch he walks to the car, where he deposits the shoes and books under the rug on the back seat. He pauses for a few seconds, becoming aware that he forgot to have the lock fixed on the back door. 'Ah, they'll be alright,' he decides. 'If somebody was goin' to rob a car, they'd go for something better than this. Another glance at the watch. 'Plenty of time yet to have a bite to ate and, maybe a pint or two, before he'd head up to McTaggart's'.

Ned has arrived in Youghal, in plenty of time for his appointment at eight o'clock. He guides his trusty reliable Bluebird down to its usual destination and parks behind Nicky's car. He, too, registers mild surprise, and is a little puzzled that there are no other cars parked on the street. Anyway, he was expecting it to be quiet. On nice evenings like this people usually go for drives up the coast.

Youghal is a very old, historic town, nestling on the estuary of the famous Blackwater River, a river world renowned for its salmon fishing. The town itself is steeped in myth and story, situated on the Cork-Waterford border. It is a fishing town, and has an attractive beach where crowds congregate in the summer. Years ago, when the trains were operating, day-trippers commuted from Cork City in large numbers. The main street traverses the town from east to west. The inhabitants are proud of their town and, it is, without doubt, an attractive place to reside, especially so for those with an innate love of the sea. On film, that great sea-faring epic, "Moby Dick," starring Gregary Peck, was shot in Youghal. It was one of the first large budget films ever made in Ireland, and it proved a marvellous local tourist attraction.

However, the town and its history holds no interest for Ned on this particular evening. Having made sure that his car is properly locked – not that anyone would run away with it – he makes his way in the general direction of McTaggart's public house. Listening to the car radio driving in, he heard a doctor say how much overweight people tended to be nowadays. It will be the cause of a major health problem in years to come, the doctor forecast, particularly with diabetes. Prostate cancer, and other diseases that men are prone to get worried Ned. As he watched the people walking along he concluded that the doctor was spot on. He wondered now had he a touch of diabetes himself. He noticed he was thirsty and peeing a lot, lately. 'Anyway, I'll put all that behind me. I have more on my mind right now,' he decides, as he contemplates the night ahead. 'I wonder what will she be like?,' he repeats the mantra one more time. He nips in to Ryan's pub and slapping the money down on the counter addresses Fat Dickie, the barman. 'Dickie, give me a half Paddy, for the love of God.' An elderly fisherman – a fixture of the place – sitting on a barstool, greets him.

'Hello there, Ned.'

'How are you Billy? You're lookin' well.'

Dickie sets the whiskey down on the counter. 'There you are.'

'Thanks.' Ned pockets the change.

'Great weather for the farmers,' Billy probes.

'Great for the fishermen too,' Ned reminds him.

'When you see a red sky in the west, the weather is

settled,' Billy solemnly pronounces, as if this were a statement of some profound importance.

'You're right, you're right. We could be in for a right spell of weather. We're due wan.'

'Twas bad enough, long enough.'

'There's a bit of a change forecast,' Fat Dickie announces.

'Not at all.' Billy contradicts him – fishermen are supposed to know those things — 'not with that sky.' He turns his attention back to Ned. 'And how are you all out in Glentallagh?'

'Never better,' Ned replies.

'I wasn't up that way in a long time. Not since the oul' legs came against me. Wouldn't be able for them hills now. Tell me this, and tell me no more, did you meet up with the right little woman yet?'

'No, not yet.'

'Be God, that's a show. Or Nicky?'

'The same.'

'What am I goin' to do with ye at all? Sure a house is not a home without the little woman. Isn't that right, Dickie?'

'Don't know. I didn't locate wan myself yet.'

'Oh sure, that's right. You kick with the left foot.'

'What are you sayin'? What did you mean by that?' Fat Dickie angrily demands.

'Nothing, nothing, nothing.'

Ned gulps down the whiskey in one go, not wishing to get involved in conversation – especially the current one. 'I'll be off then. Goodluck!'

Billy is openly disappointed at this outcome, fully expecting the offer of a drink. 'Heh, take it easy. What's your hurry?' He hops down and almost topples over as his legs collapse under him. He grabs hold of the counter. 'I have something to tell you,' he shouts. 'Hey, come back!' But Ned is out the door. 'Feck you!'... Holding himself up he gazes at the closed door. 'That's not like him,' he sadly proclaims. 'you'd think the divil was on his tail.'

Turning back to Dickie he thumps the counter with his fist. 'I'll tell you wan thing; the days of the ould dacency are gone. That's all I have to say.'

Every time Ned visits Youghal he's reminded of Joan Kiely. He's reminded of the times they danced in the Red Barn, a dancehall a few miles outside the town. When Joan rejected Ned, part of the enjoyment and laughter in his life was extinguished for ever. 'What's the use; you have to take the rough with the smooth,' he says out loud. A passing woman looks at him with curiosity. He goes into an off-license and purchases a naggin bottle of Power's Gold Label whiskey, which he stuffs down into his breast pocket. Feeling fortified, and with some trepidation, he head's for McTaggart's

Breda is also approaching Youghal, from the opposite direction. She is tense and apprehensive, wondering what the night holds in store. 'But what else could she do?' She conjured up the mental image of the loneliness and desolation of spending another winter on her own. 'I hope he's a decent and honourable man,' she thought, 'and not the kind of chancer Nancy felt he might turn out to be.' Nancy knew about those things. Maybe that's why she felt so anxious right now. 'At least she's comin' in so I'll not be on my own too long. ... This could be an awful big step I'm taking so I have to be careful. God, why am I such an idiot where men are concerned?' she asked herself bitterly. The closeness and intimacy of married life didn't appeal to her all that much. 'Still, what do all other women do? I can't be any different.... I'll have to do something with myself. I can't keep on like this. If her father could see her now what would he think?' Her parents never encouraged her to mix much. She never did. Was that why she felt uncomfortable with some people? She often felt the people around considered her behaviour odd. Maybe her parents felt it was the duty of the eldest daughter to stay at home and look after them when they got old and feeble. Was it that her fate was sealed the day she came in to this world? 'She drew the short straw – isn't that what they called it.' She rounded a bend and saw the lights of the town in the distance. She slowed down and felt like turning back, but she knew there was no going back now. She felt her heart pump a little faster.

"Whatever you do talk to him," Nancy said. Maybe he'll be an easy man to talk to – someone like the postman The postman was happy, now that he had made friends with Glen.... He was starting to behave in a peculiar way lately, though. 'Is there something coming over him by any chance?' She noticed he was beginning to smile at her in a strange way. And what did he mean by – "Maybe we should get to know each other better?' Didn't she know him well enough already. Then the way he winks his eye.

'Is it a little affliction he have, I wonder. I hope this fella inside will have no affliction.'

At this moment in time Nancy is swinging her car out the gateway of her home, en-route to the rendezvous. She is glad to be getting away from the tension-filled atmosphere of the house. Her mother still hadn't returned. Her father quizzed her as to where she was going.

"There's plenty for you to be doing around here. What are you goin' out for anyhow? – seeing that the big romance is finished. You're on the shelf now, so you might as well resign yourself to it." How could he be so insensitive, cruel and ignorant. She still felt emotionally shattered. That man had no grain of sympathy, no human kindness in his make-up. She hit back hard though. She told him he was the one who should stay inside; that his liver was banjaxed from drinking alcohol. 'Look at yourself in the mirror; your puffed-up face is after turning yellow.' He didn't like that. She knew, at this very minute, he was down at the dressing-table, studying his face from all angles. She acknowledged to herself, that her mother was a long-suffering saint. She should leave him altogether and be done with it. She knew a lot about "Jimeen the Rat." She knew she had a half-sister in Midleton who strongly resembled herself. She knew he was the best garage man around at turning the clocks back in second-hand cars. She could go on. "At least you have your folks to talk to when you come home in the evenings," Breda said. Little did she know.

She was glad she was meeting Breda this evening, even if the circumstances generated mixed feelings in her. 'Imagine Breda is meeting a man and I'm the gooseberry! Why am I such a selfish bitch?' she asked herself in disgust. Breda was her one shining beacon; she was warm, true and honest. There is no hypocrisy in her. She knew she was always welcome in Breda's house. Just for some reason, she never even contemplated the very notion of Breda meeting someone. 'What's this guy going to turn out like? That's the six marker. It's surprising she didn't confide in me about what she intended doing – replying to this "Lonely Heart" type of ad. on the paper.' They kept few secrets. 'She was probably depressed and lonely over there some night. That was it. Probably a bit confused.' The same way as she herself felt right now. 'I'll have to put on a brave face, anyhow,' she vowed, as moving on to the main road she revved up the engine.

Chapter Seven

McTaggart's

Ned Has arrived a little early at the small snug-like lounge of McTaggart's licensed premises. He has bought himself a pint of Guinness and a half measure of whiskey.

The place is sparsely furnished: three small tables, with strong wooden chairs, occupy the floor area. A few high-backed bar stools are strategically placed around by the walls. The entrance is through a dimly lit hallway, top left, leading in from the public bar and the street outside. Sunken wall-lights brighten up the room. There is a serving hatch – which opens and closes – top right, in front of which is a small counter on which the orders are placed. Various posters, advertising alcoholic drinks, are positioned on the walls: "Guinness for Strength, Power's Gold Label, Smithwick's Ale, Bushmill's Whiskey." A couple of "No Smoking" signs are pinned up around the place. The room, obviously, is very basic and little used.

Ned, in his good Sunday clothes, new cap and polished boots, is standing centre. He takes a good swig out of the pint of Guinness and places the glass down on one of the tables. Being on his own, and to calm his nerves, he had lit up a cigarette which he now stubs out. He looks around for somewhere to deposit the butt-end; he settles by dropping it down the back of one of the "No Smoking" signs. He waves his hands in the air to disperse the smoke. After first looking down the hall, he takes the naggin bottle of whiskey out of his pocket and tops up the whiskey glass. With glass in hand, in thought, he strides about the room, glancing anxiously towards the hallway.

Breda enters and, excited looking, Ned crosses to greet her. Breda is wearing a blouse, skirt and jumper, and a loose jacket. She has on low-heeled shoes and has a beret on her head. Her hair is hanging loose. The skirt she has on comes down well below the knees. She hasn't applied any 'make-up.' She is carrying a large handbag. Her clothes appear outdated and give her an unwarranted, staid, matronly appearance. Despite this, it is apparent that Breda possesses an underlying attractiveness.

Ned contemplates giving Breda a kiss on the cheek – the same as he sees on television — but he feels too shy and awkward for this. He stretches out his hand, saying, 'Hello …. Breda?'

Breda responds, shaking his hand. 'Hello Ned.'

'You were able to make it after all. I was … I was getting a bit worried there.'

'Sorry I'm a little late. The traffic was heavy.'

'It's okay, it's okay.' He pulls out a chair. 'Here, sit down, sit down. You're right, the bloody traffic is gone to hell altogether. No comfort on the roads anymore. Anyway, you got here in one piece, that's the important thing. And I'm real glad to see you. What will you have to drink?'

'It's alright, I don't drink.'

Ned looks somewhat disappointed. 'Oh, you don't drink. Sure come on and have something anyhow. Our first time meeting.'

'I know .... It all feels a little strange. I'll have a bottle of lemonade then – or orange, or anything.'

'Right. We'll settle on an orange then.' He crosses and taps on the service hatch with a coin. It opens, but is not large enough for the bar-tender to be seen.. Lowering his head he orders the drink. Breda is glancing about as she is not familiar with the interior of public houses. 'Did you have a job finding this place?' Ned turns around and asks.

'No, no, you gave good instructions. I know the town fairly well.'

The drink is duly served up, which he pays for, saying 'Thanks.' He crosses to the table and places the glass of orange in front of Breda. 'Here you are.'

'Thank you.'

'Would you like a Kit-Kat or something, to go with that?'

'No, I'm fine, this is grand.'

'Maybe you don't like the cut of this place? I should have said the hotel above. We could always –'

'No, it's alright.' She looks about again. 'It's nice and quiet, like you said.'

'Yeh, it's quiet alright. Tuesdays and Wednesdays are the quietest days of the week in the pub trade.'

'You seem to know a bit about it?'

'You pay to learn, and I've contributed a fair bit. Be God I have.'

'Oh, you have!'

'Well, you know how it is?' He sits down opposite Breda. 'Thanks for comin', anyhow. I was hoping you wouldn't get second thoughts. That's what was runnin' through my head.'

'We kind of broke the ice over the phone. I was wondering afterwards should we have talked a little longer?'

'That's what I was thinkin' myself. But what difference!' He clinks his glass against Breda's, toasting, 'Good-luck, then. And here's to whatever might lie in store.'

'Yes.' There is an awkward silence, as both are suddenly at a loss for words. 'I never did something like this before – made an arrangement like this,' Breda says.

'Me neither.'

'There's a first time for everything, I suppose ... Well, anyhow, here we are.'

'Yeh, here we are.' Another pause, before Ned blurts out, 'At least you didn't turn on your heels and run out the door when you saw me.'

'You look exactly as I had you pictured in my mind.'

'You look different to what I thought you would – better looking, mind.'

'Go on now, with your flattery.'

'No, I mean it. The minute I saw you.'

'I always like to speak the plain truth. That's the way I am.'

'That is the plain truth.'

'Anyway, none of us fell down with shock, so we'll leave it at that. Maybe some people who do this kind of thing exchange photos before they meet. "Farmer seeks woman with a combine harvester. Please send photo of combine harvester."'

'Oh I heard that wan,' Ned smiles. 'Not much corn where I come from, so that wouldn't enter into it.'

'Ned Power, you said. What part are you from, then?'

'Glentallagh is the name of the townland. It's not too far from Midleton.'

'That's not a hundred miles away. How do you spell it?'

'G-l-e-n-t-a-l-l-a-g-h.'

'Ned Power, from Glentallagh, Midleton.'

'And yourself?'

'A place called Redferne, Dungarvan.' She spells, 'R-e-d-f-e-r-n-e. It's more-or-less between Dungarvan and Youghal – closer, I suppose, to Dungarvan. It's a Scottish sounding name, isn't it?'

'Is it?'

'My name is Kane, as I told you. People think it's Keane, but that I just call it Kane. You know, the way people call tea tay.'

'We're not too far from each other at all, then.'

'No, not too far. Do you know anyone from Redferne? Breda inquires.

'I had a dale with a man from that side once. I'll never forget it. Was there ever anyone belonging to you a cattle jobber?'

'No, no, not that I know of.'

'Good, because this fella was a right bastard.' Ned is vehement as he continues. 'He took me for a ride, no two ways about it. He had these cattle at the mart that were drugged to keep 'em quiet. When I bought 'em I thought they were dead placid. Walked up into the lorry, no bother. But be the lovin' jasus when I got 'em home they went stone mad! They'd go for you bald-headed; tore across fields, ditches, the river, the old railway track, halfways round the parish. I'll tell you wan thing, them cattle will stay with me for ever.'

'And that man too, I imagine. You couldn't be up to most of them fellas. They know every trick.'

'You can say that again. He had the head of a rogue, so I should have known. A curly head like a shorthorn bull.'

'I dealt with a few of them fellas myself.'

'You did?' Ned sounds surprised.

'I had to, I had no choice. A few of them are alright now, to be fair. They helped me out. You see, my father got a stroke and was laid up for years. I was the only one left to look after him. My mother passed away when we were small, and my two sisters are married abroad.'

'Oh, I see.'

'He's dead now over six months. Maybe it's too early to be doing something like this?'

'Not a bit of it. So, you're on your own then? All alone.'

'All alone is right. Land is making good money, and people tell me I should sell up and get out. But I don't know. It's my home, and what would I go at then. I don't know anything else.'

'That's it; that's the problem alright,' Ned agrees. You're kind of stuck with it no matter what way you turn.'

'It's an awful thing, a stroke. One of the worst things there is, I'd say. Getting a heavy man in and out of bed, and up and down to the toilet is no joke, I can tell you that. My back was starting to give me no end of trouble.'

'Twas hard goin' alright, no two ways about it. 'Twas a harsh sentence.'

'I knew by the look on his face that it broke his heart what he was putting me through. The poor man couldn't do anything about it. None of us could.' She gestures with futility. 'That's life, I suppose.'

'No let-up at all?'

'Very little. The neighbours were good enough, but the house is fairly isolated. Now and then I got a break from it. I used pay a woman to come in and give me a hand to get him on the wheelchair, and back to bed again.'

'Your health is your wealth, no matter what way you look at it.'

'You can be certain sure of it. And people worry about all kinds of silly things. Anyway, he was my father and he was company. Now that he's gone it's a lonely station there on your own. That's why I'm here this evening.

But don't think because I am here that we're goin' to end up walking up the aisle. You know what I mean? Might as well be straight about it.'

'Oh yeh. Oh I know that. Sure we just met.'

'It's a big decision, what we're on about. You have to be sure it's going to work out.'

'It might work out the finest.'

'We'll see. I've been waiting a good few years now, so I'm not going to rush into something. There can be worse things than feeling lonely and sorry for yourself.... Now you know my story. Tell me about yourself then?'

'Well, to be honest, there's not a hell of a lot to tell. I have only the wan sister who's married above in Galway. Ah, she moved up a bit in the world and got high notions about herself. She rarely, if ever, darkens the door now. It's not good enough for her anymore. You know how snobby some people can get – even your own.'

'Only the two of you?'

'That's all. Like yourself, I live alone. It can get you down at times, no doubt about it. A body needs a bit of company, and that's the truth of it. Lookin' at the four walls. Sure, Christ above, 'tis enough to drive you cracked. You end up talkin' to yourself and behavin' kind of quare.'

'Have you a big place?'

'No, it's not that big, but then again, it's not that small – forty three acres.'

'That's not too bad. There's only thirty one at home.'

'Put 'em together and you'd be goin' somewhere,' Ned enthuses.

'What's the land like? Is it sound?' she inquires.

'Well, a little on the high side. Grazing land, like. It's powerful dry ground for winterin' cattle.'

'A comfortable house, I suppose?'

'Oh God yes, a tidy snug house. It could do with a lick of paint, maybe. What it badly needs now is a woman's touch. Sure a woman can work wonders around a place.'

Breda studies Ned's face with some intensity. 'You're in your late forties, you said. To tell you the honest-to-God truth, I'd take you to be a little more. I hope you don't mind me saying that now? That's just the way I am. I like to come out with things.'

'I like straight talk meself. You see, some people age a bit quicker than others. It's a little family failin' we have.'

'It doesn't matter. Have you any more failings though, I wonder?'

'Jasus, Breda, is there anyone perfect? Even the Man above lost his temper and bet the people out of the temple. The guards never hauled me in for anything. And I think I'm sound enough in wind and limb.'

'Thankfully my own health is pretty good too. You don't over-indulge in the drink, I hope.'

'Sure when I'm out I like a few. You have to be sociable, you know what I mean?'

'I don't mind a man havin' the odd drink. But my father,

God rest him, always warned me to be careful of any man who drank too much. "'Twas the ruination of too many places," he said. He was able to name several farms that were drank out. The poor wife and children hungry, and the husband below in the pub and he not able to put a leg under himself.'

'That's a common enough story alright.'

''Tis a serious story. Anyway, like I said, finding myself on my own is the reason I'm here tonight.'

'The very same as myself.'

'Those long winter nights, without a soul to talk to, can be a heavy cross. Especially those nights from mid-November on, when it's dark at half-four. That leaves you with a long night to ponder.'

'And another thing,' Ned stresses emphatically, 'it's deadly dangerous nowadays for a woman to be alone in the country. There are people goin' girl, who'd slit your throat and think nothin' of it. Money for drugs is what they want, and they don't care how they get it. Have you a gun in the house?'

Breda is slightly aghast at this suggestion. 'God no! What would I be doing with a gun?'

'A pity. People know I keep a double-barrel handy. It's your only man.'

'I have a very good watch-dog, so I feel safe enough. Sometimes alright, I imagine I hear noises outside at night'

'There you are! See what I mean?'

'I'd get up and put on the kettle. I'd be sitting there drinking tea, at three o'clock in the morning maybe. Listening to the wind moaning on the gable-end, like the banshee herself. I heard her wanse, too.'

It's Ned's turn to look puzzled. 'You did?'

'Off in the distance. Put the shivers up and down your spine.'

'I thought the electricity got rid of the banshee and the like. What you heard now, was an old vixen fox.'

'I don't think so.'

''You can be sure of it. Or a randy oul' tom-cat on the prowl. What you badly need is a couple of Alsations. They're the boys to have.'

'You know, no matter how you look at it, it's hard on a woman.'

'That's what I'm saying.'

'Everyway. What I mean is, I'm not like you; I couldn't ramble off down to the pub on my own, for a drink or a game of cards. What would happen? The men would be trying to get off with me.'

'What!'

'Well, wouldn't they? What do you think?... Come on?'

Ned is a trifle perplexed by this turn of events. 'Ah.... well....I don't know.' He scratches his chin. 'I suppose some fella might chance his arm, alright.'

'They'd think I was a good thing – the parish bike. I know what they'd say; there would be stories flyin' around about me. "That immoral woman down the lane."'

'Things are not like that anymore. Attitudes have changed about… about those kind of things.'

'That's another thing I want to talk to you about: I told you I spent all those years looking after my father. That means I never went out much. It means I have no real experience of men…. if you know what I mean? I don't know like….like how I'd be with a man. That aspect worries me. How about you?'

Ned's eyes have widened. 'How about me?'

'You know? Have you much experience of women?…. You know?….that other part of it?'

Ned gulps at the Guinness, spilling some down his front, devouring half the pint in one swallow. 'What… what exactly do you mean, like?'

Nancy enters.

'We'll talk again,' Breda says quickly.

Chapter Eight

Time to Ponder

Foxy jumps out of the bed and, looking back, gives Trish a playful slap on the buttock.

'God, you're any man's fancy, you know that?'

'I'm sure. Now look what you've done. I'll set fire to the bed.'

'I'll take the dogs out for awhile,' he announces, pulling on his jeans, shirt, socks and runners. He heads out to the yard where the dogs jump up against him and whimper with excitement.

After a few minutes, when Foxy and the dogs are gone, Trish slides out of bed, revealing once again her voluptuous figure. She moves across to the dressing table and her myriad assortment of potions, creams, eye-shadow, hair-colouring and lipstick. She wants to be prepared for whatever the night holds in store. Hopefully they'd stay in. 'Christ, it was all hours when they got home last night.'

However, she knew well how unpredictable Foxy could be: one minute he'd ask, "What's on the old telly?" The next minute it would be, "Come on, we'll go out for feck sake." They had been together now – apart from some blips – for a good number of years. Whether by accident or design, they had no offspring. Foxy, possibly, didn't want the constraint of children. Trish, true to her nature, felt different, but things just seemed to drift on.

They had moved to Liverpool at one stage. He

worked on the buildings, she worked in a factory. It was an experience they didn't particularly enjoy, and they ended up back in Youghal after eight months. Foxy reckoned he learned a good deal about his trade, during this stint in Liverpool. She always knew that he wouldn't be happy in the city. She was well aware that he craved the freedom of the countryside: to ramble at will with the dogs, the Blackwater river to fish, Morgan's racing stables to ride out the horses on the weekends. She also knew he wasn't as faithful as he might have been whilst they were away. She acknowledged that she was no shrinking violet herself in that respect. Overall, taking the good with the bad, she was happy enough now.

In various ways Trish looked up to Foxy, realizing that mentally he was pretty sharp. He was a diverse type of individual, who always had her puzzled in some ways: the odd night he'd stay in he'd spend it alone in the bedroom, reading or listening to music; the next night he'd say, "You might as well be dead if you don't go out among the people." Out they'd go where, more likely than not, he'd drink too much, act the idiot and get into rows. This resulted in confrontation with the police on a couple of occasions. He also attempted to play the guitar and compose songs. She thought he was fairly good, but other people said he was useless. She countered this by saying, 'Geniuses are only recognised when they're dead.' Both of them knew a good cross section of people, in the town and the neighbouring hinterland. Occasionally, she was asked why she stayed with Foxy. "Didn't she know what he was like?" There was another side to him and she felt she knew the various strands to his personality. Life is strange, she reasoned, and who knows what binds people together.

Lately she worried though, about the amount of drink and other drugs he appeared to be getting addicted to. He laughed this off however, so maybe it was nothing to be too concerned about. A lot of the young people they knew behaved in a similar fashion. The weekends were starting to feel less carefree, she noticed. Could it be the amount of fights she witnessed recently? There was something different in the air and she felt uneasy, and yet unable to relate what it was, exactly, that made her feel this way. 'When there was less money about things were happier,' she thought. 'Ah, to hell with it! Pretty soon, she reminded herself, they'd be headin' out to Tenerife. This kept her spirits up. Probably another drink-sodden fortnight, like last year in Las Palmas, but what about it? 'There'll be half a dozen of us in it, and Christ we'll let it rip! They're all good fun, aren't they? –every one of 'em. Feck it, you only live the once.'

Up at The Deli restaurant Nicky had sat down to a formidable fry which consisted of a large portion of chips, eggs, rashers, sausages, black and white puddings, liver, a lamb chop and a pint of milk. Silly things like cholesterol and calories didn't trouble Nicky. Nearing the end of the meal now, he glances out the window and becomes aware of the three hefty dogs practically pulling Foxy along the footpath. He smiles, saying to himself, 'Feckin' idiot.' He belches a few times, mops up the last of the greasy chips, pays for the meal and gives the waitress fifty cent as a tip. Going out the door, turning left, he almost bumps into a large member of the Garda Siochana. Automatically he says, 'Sorry.' The response he gets is a curt 'Watch it.' Peeved, looking after the guard, he mumbles 'Bollocks!' On the grapevine, Nicky heard there was a right whore's ghost of a young garda after being posted to Youghal. Someone who'd "summons" his own mother. As he looked after this individual's departing frame he wondered was that him. It was.

Pausing, looking at her image in the mirror, Trish questions what she's doing – 'Surely they'd stay in tonight. Not two nights in a row.' Foxy arrives back with the panting dogs, feeds them again, barges inside and announces, 'Come on, we'll go out for awhile.'
'Clint Eastwood is on the telly,' she reminds him hopefully. "The Unforgiven." 'It's supposed to be really good.' Westerns appealed to him.
'I saw it before,' he replies. 'It's good alright.' He proceeds to change his sweat-soiled shirt. 'A fairly violent film. You could stay in and watch it yourself.'
'I don't like violent films. You know that.'
'Sure come on out, then.'

No use in arguing now. The obligatory glass of Black and White whiskey is consumed. This, to give them that extra lift. Cheaper too, purchasing it by the bottle at the supermarket

It is a goodish walk to the centre of the town, but at least he always had enough savvy to let the car behind. If he were spotted driving, with the possibility of having drink taken, the guards would come down on him like a ton of bricks – and he knew it. They looked an incongruous pair as they trudged along; he, with a guitar case slung over his shoulder and Trish, face heavily made-up, scantily clad, in a brief mini-skirt, looking exceedingly like a lady of the night.

'I feel bet. Why are we hittin' out tonight?' she asks, as they walk along.
'I'm a bit low in gear,' he replies.

'God, I thought you said you don't need it?'
'I don't. Don't worry, I can live without it. Wait'll you see.'

Chapter Nine

A Small Deception

Nancy is looking well. She is dressed in a navy blue trouser-suit, with matching accessories. On seeing the others she feigns complete surprise. Breda reacts in a similar fashion.

Nancy says, 'Breda! God above!'

'Janey!, Nancy!' Breda responds.

Nancy puts on a broad smile. 'Of all people, I never expected to see you here.'

'I never expected you to walk in that door either,' Breda adds. Ned and herself are now standing. With a gesture of her outstretched arm she introduces Ned. 'This is Ned Power. Ned, meet Nancy Clery.'

Nancy reaches out her hand. 'Nice to meet you, Ned.'

Ned shakes her hand. 'The same. How are you?'

'Life has its little surprises,' Breda continues. 'Imagine you coming in here.'

Ned looks from one to the other. 'You seem to know each other well?'

'That's an under-statement,' Nancy says.

'It is,' Breda confirms.

'Anyway, will you have a drink with us?'

'Ah no, it's alright.'

'Come on, what is it?'

'Thanks, then. I have a touch of a pain in my side. I decided to nip in here for a brandy and port. Hope I'm not intruding?'

'No, no, not at all,' Breda quickly replies. 'Here, sit down.' They both seat themselves.

'Right, I'll get that then.' Ned still looks a little flustered. 'A brandy and port,' he repeats. 'Hennessy, is it?'

'Yes, thanks.'

He crosses and orders the drink, going through the same procedure as before.

'I can't get over bumping into you; in here, of all places,' Breda says.

Nancy winks back, 'I only dropped in because it's such a quiet spot. It's a bit of a dump, I know.'

Breda continues the charade. 'Were you working late?'

Glancing behind, Nancy grins, 'No, I had a bit of business in town.'

Ned turns round, 'So you know each other really well, then?'

'We live in the same locality,' Nancy informs him.

'That's a good wan alright.' He crosses with the drink. 'Here you are.' He has got himself another whiskey and ordered another pint.

'Thanks again. I think I must have a touch of an ulcer. This mixture seems to do me good. I know I'm breaking in on you now – on your chat?'

'You're not,' Breda assures her.

'You're alright, the night's long.' He gives himself a shake, places the whiskey on the table. 'Well, first things first; I must water the horse.' He heads off down the hallway.

'That's wan way of putting it,' Nancy smiles. She reaches forward, inquiring with some urgency. 'Well? How are you getting on?'

'Alright, I'd say. Bit early to tell.'

'Is he okay? Come on? What's he like?'

'What do you think of him?'

'Don't mind what I think. What do you think?'

'He seems sound enough.'

'Good.'

'What do you make of him?' Breda asks anxiously.

'Give me a chance.'

'First impressions, like?'

'Well, you'd know he was hewn from rough stone. But what about that. You don't judge a book by the cover. The important thing is, are ye hittin' it off okay?'

'He drinks a fair bit, I'd say. I don't like that.'

''It gives him a bit of courage, maybe.'

'I don't know. He has a fair few in already. Notice his breath; he smells like a brewery.'

'What's he like to talk to?'

'He talks away. I mean he's alright. I never expected him to be perfect.'

'Where's he from?'

'Glentallagh. It's up near Midleton.'

'That's not too far.'

'What age would you put on him?'

'Around the fifty-five mark, I'd say.'

'I was thinkin' the same.'

'If you feel you're starting off okay, that's something. Has he a big place? Did you ask him?'

'Forty three acres.'

'With today's values that's worth a tidy sum.'

'I suppose. It's hilly, he said.'

'You know, I'd say he's decent enough. He strikes me as the kind who's not afraid to put his hand in his pocket.'

'What'll I say if he wants to meet me again?'

'Wait an' see how it goes. It's early days yet.' Finger to lips, 'Sssh!'

Ned returns, finishing zipping up his fly. 'That's better. That Guinness would run through you! I always say 'tis a small world – the way people bump into each other.'

'Ned is from Glentallagh, Midleton,' Breda says.

'Glentallagh,' Nancy repeats. 'I knew a girl from around there once. Her boyfriend got killed off a motorcycle.

She took it really bad. In fact she was so broken-hearted she entered a convent.'

'Was she a Cahill by any chance?', Ned questions.

'Yeh, I think that was it. Yes, Cahill – I'm nearly sure.'

'I know who you're talkin' about now. 'Twas a sad accident, no two ways about it. But then, all accidents are sad. Them motorbikes, though, are death traps altogether.'

'Do you know her? Nancy queries.

'I know her to see. I know her father well. He have a cure for the shingles – Cahill's blood.'

'It surprised me when I heard what she'd done.'

'She didn't stick the convent too long. Ah sure, you don't somersault into the nuns. You have to be cut out for that job.'

'She left?'

'She ran off with the gardener. The last I heard of her she had triplets.'

'God Almighty!' Breda exclaims.

''Twouldn't surprise me. I couldn't picture her in a convent', Nancy smiles. 'She was wild, she was mad out.'

'Know anyone else from the Glentallagh side,' Ned asks.

''I know yourself now, don't I.'

'And maybe that's enough. Once seen never forgotten! Breda asked you there were you working late – so you're workin' locally then?'

'The American factory outside.'

'Oh be God! I hear people are pullin' powerful money out of that place.'

'The money's good, but you're expected to work hard for it'

'It's great for the town and the area. What would you say I work at now? Maybe Breda told you?'

'No, she didn't.'

The alcohol is lowering Ned's guard a little and he is becoming more talkative than normal. 'Come on then, what would you think? Have a guess?'

Nancy decides to play along. 'Are you a vet?'

Ned scratches his chin. 'No, no.'

'An inspector with the Department of Agriculture?'

'Jasus no! Not wan of that shower.'

'An A.I. man,? Nancy adds slyly.

'An A.I. man! An A.I. man!' Ned is amused. 'No, be God. I lave that job to the bull himself. But you're getting close.'

'Don't tell me you're a farmer?'

'You hit the nail on the head. All my life slavin' an' draggin' on the side of a hill.'

'Slaving is right,' Breda elaborates. 'Out in hail, rain and snow.'

'Where did you two run into each other?' Nancy queries

'We met in a kind of round-about way,' Ned says, unfazed. 'Are you a married woman yourself? You are, no doubt. Just waiting around for himself to show?'

'No, no, I'm not married.'

'There's someone on the sideline then?'

'There's no one on the sideline either.'

'That's surprising, for a fine cut of a girl like you. Plenty of men up in that factory.' Ned is standing, fresh pint glass in hand.

'They all seem to prefer younger models.'

'There can be better stuff in the ould wans – more reliable

'The ould wans aren't appreciated anymore.'

'That's it, that's it exactly,' Ned exclaims. 'It's only the youth they want now. That's the sad part of it. And be God, I'll tell you wan thing, the years can catch up on you before you know it. Then, when you look back, you wonder how they all went so fast.' He shakes his head philosophically. 'Don't know where they all went. And the older you get the faster they go. Anyway, to hell with it! Talkin' about years; what age would you say I am?'

'What age? God, you're all questions Ned.'

'The truth now? What would you say?'

'Oh, I imagine you're about sixty-five.'

Ned looks dumbstruck. 'What? Sixty-five...?'

'Around that.'

'Sixty-five…'

'Only joking. In your mid-forties, are you?'

He is much relieved. 'You're spot on! You're a good wan alright! You're a bit of a sport, I'd say.' He turns to Breda, palms outstretched. 'There you are now,'

'Maybe the whiskey is making you look younger; it's making you talk younger, anyhow.'

'Isn't it great to be young at heart. What do you think, Nancy? Forget the cares of the world. It wont make wan bit of difference in the long run. We'll all go out the same way.'

'No use in speeding it up,' Breda upbraids him.

'When you're dead an' gone very few will give a damn.'

'You've put your finger on it,' Nancy agrees. 'It's when you're dead and gone though, that they'll all say nice things about you. They'll say, Ned ….sorry, what's your second name again?'

'Power.'

'They'll say, "Ned Power will be sadly missed. He was a sound neighbour – the best in the world. Sure the poor craotar always had a great heart, and a kind word for everyone. And another thing, he was a dacent man in the pub."'

'That would be a nice epitaph to have,' Breda cynically repeats, "He was a dacent man in the pub."'

'It wouldn't matter much then, what the hell they'd say,'

Ned responds.

'I wonder is drink available in the next world?' Nancy jokes. 'A pint of Guinness and a half wan, Saint Peter please, when you're ready.'

Nicky suddenly emerges from the hallway. He is dressed in a similar fashion to Ned, except that his suit is brown. The hat with feather – tilted a little to one side now – remains in place. He stands back, taking in the scene.

'Christ, Nicky!' Ned exclaims loudly, in a surprised tone.

Nicky winks the eye and points the finger, 'Ned, I knew I'd find you. This is me fourth pub, but I knew I'd track you down.'

'Nicky boy, it looks like I can't get away from you.'

'I always thought wan woman would be enough for any man, but aren't you the lucky fellow with two. And two fine girls they are at that.'

'I suppose you want a drink?'

'It wouldn't go astray.'

'You tracked me down is right. Meet Breda Kane and Nancy Clery. This fella here is Nicky Daly.

Chapter Ten

Drama at Glentallagh

Since Nicky left home events have taken an unexpected turn. Mary and Paddy had sat down and finished the supper Nicky had earlier prepared. Paddy then brought the cutlery across to the sink. Neither of the two were very mobile, and Nicky assured them he would do the cleaning and washing-up when he got back. He always attended to this chore; in fact, a great deal of his time was now spent in looking after the old folk. Though they hadn't a very big appetite, they enjoyed the meal. After supper their usual routine was to sit around and watch their twenty-year-old television until after the nine o'clock news, then make their way slowly up to the bedroom. Paddy found it necessary to use one crutch, as his right leg was painful.

Nicky said he would be home early. But they knew Nicky, and that his "early" could be tomorrow morning. That was their biggest worry, as they were fearful something might happen to them during the course of the night. This nightmare scenario suddenly became a probability: shortly after the meal Mary started to complain of a pain in her left side. Paddy did his best to pacify her, but the pain showed no sign of abating. He started to panic then. "What the hell am I goin' to do now?" he exclaimed. "That bloody young-fella is never here when he's wanted. Blast his soul!" He implored her, "how are you now? Are you better?" "No I'm not, Paddy," she plaintively wailed. "Ring for Nellie. Her number is wrote in the front of the book."

Nellie, a retired nurse, is one of their neighbours. She is a big-hearted person, who is constantly kept busy attending to cases like this. Some farmers even sought her advice about sick animals. People from all around valued her opinion first, before they went any further. Nellie is definitely the most popular person in the whole parish. She has a reputation for kindness, and never makes a big issue out of any situation.

Mary lay prone on her bed, groaning. It wasn't long before Nellie arrived on the scene. Prior to her coming, Paddy had asked Mary should he ring for the priest. This caused her to wail out, "Oh God no! You don't think I'm goin' to die – or do you?' "No, no," he replied. "I just thought you might like to make your peace. We'll all have to go sometime." "I don't want to go tonight," she cried out, louder still.

When Nellie arrived she was accompanied by her husband, Mick. He was her regular driver on occasions like this, as Nellie was nervous of travelling alone at night. It was early evening yet, but there was no guarantee how long she might be in the house. Nellie was quickly up in the bedroom, anxiously followed by Paddy. Nellie's very presence alone re-assured Mary and, for some reason, she began to feel better already. Nellie asked her where the pain was, and said it would be worse if it were on the right side. She asked Mary had she been to the bathroom, and Mary said she had, a couple of times. "You might have a little touch of food poisoning," Nellie said, in her relaxed, soothing, hypnotic tone of voice. "What had you for your tea? Was everything fresh?' "You wouldn't know what that fella would throw up to you," Paddy said, still tetchy over Nicky's absence. In truth, one of Nicky's redeeming features was that he always tried to have something presentable for every meal. Nellie was thinking, however, that maybe he had come in from the yard and handled the food without washing his hands. Hygiene, of that type, may not be too high up on his priority list. Being aware that Mary was well on in years, Nellie insisted that the doctor would have to be called out, just to be on the safe side. After all, if something untoward were to happen during the night it would leave Nellie in a very compromised situation. Doctor O'Leary duly arrived in quick time and, after attending to Mary, announced that there was nothing urgent required. He left some powders, one to be taken every three hours. Tucking away his sixty euro call-out charge he told Paddy she should be fine by morning.

Before Nellie and Mick left their own house, Alice Carmundy had been a visitor. As soon as Alice heard that Mary was ill she exaggerated the fact out of all proportion. Tell Alice something and you might as well put a notice in the local paper. The telephone lines started to buzz. First Mary was unwell, then the news got round that she was really bad, finally she was on death's door. Soon the cars started to arrive at the Daly homestead. The relatives and friends started to call, to bid their last adieu to Mary and to commiserate with Paddy. This created restrained consternation with Paddy. By nature he was a shy, quiet, retiring individual. What was happening now was the very last thing he would have wished for. He knew that if Nicky had been here none of this would have happened. As soon as Mary got the turn she would have been taken, straight away, down to the doctor. He would have treated her, she would be driven home, put to bed, and that would be that. No fuss, no bother.

From her bed Mary ordered the kettle to be boiled and drink distributed. Soon people were laughing and joking and Paddy, in disbelief, was half expecting music and some sort of hooley to start up. He was out in the yard now as the small kitchen was full. He confided to his close neighbour Jackie Crowley: "they'll ate us out of house and home. There wont be a drop of whiskey left." With frustration he waves the crutch over his head. "I'll tell you wan thing, when that young fella comes home I'll redden his arse with a vamp."

Chapter Eleven

Getting to Know You

At this moment in time, Nicky is blissfully unconcerned about Mary or Paddy. Glentallagh might as well be in the North Pole. His complete attention is focussed on Breda and Nancy.

He shakes hands with both in turn, saying, 'Glad to meet you.' They respond in unison with, 'Hello.'

Ned continues, 'He's a neighbour of mine. An old buddy as well. But, like everyone, we have our arguments; we fall in and we fall out. Wan thing I can tell you for certain – and it's like your own story – I never expected to see him tonight. Be God, no. A pint, is it?'

'That'll do.'

As Ned attends to getting the drink Nicky explains. 'I said I'd scratch around till I found him. I don't know too many people in this town, and I hate proppin' up a bar on me own. You know the way it is? –the odd mag.'

Nancy moves a chair towards him. 'Here, take the weight off your feet.'

'I'm okay, I'm tired of sitting down. Where did ye meet himself?'

'Ah, we…we just started chatting,' Breda says.

'He must be getting good at the old chat-up line, seeing that he was able to rope the two of you in.'

'How about yourself? Are you good at it?, Nancy asks.

'God, no. If I was I'd be nice and snug at home with a wife, instead of lurching around this town on me own.'

Ned turns round. 'You should have said you were goin' out tonight. You never opened your mouth..'

'I know. 'Twas a spur-of-the-moment job. You get tired of looking at the four walls.'

'You live close by?' Breda inquires.

'Oh yeh.' He points at Ned. 'He lives up the road a piece. I'm down a boreen. And you know what they say? – you can live without your own, but you can't live without your neighbours. Our two farms adjoin each other.'

Nancy smiles, 'Another farmer. So you're a bachelor too?'

'So far, but I haven't given up the ghost,' Nicky declares resolutely. 'There's life in the old dog yet. Are you two… two…?'

'Spinsters,' Nancy prompts. 'I don't like that word, do you, Breda?'

'No.'

'We're single, we're unmarried.'

Nicky finds it hard to contain his enthusiasm. 'That's what I meant.' The situation has developed much better than he anticipated.

Ned returns with a tray of drink. He sets the tray down and distributes the various drinks around. 'Here we are.'

Nancy is not over-eager. 'God, Ned, I didn't want

anymore. Honest to God.'

Ned places the tray oneside. 'Get it inside you; it'll do you good.'

Breda is not over-enthusiastic either. 'I'll be full of gas after all these.'

"Here lies Ned Power," Ned states loudly, "He was a dacent man in the pub." 'Nicky, that's goin' to be on my headstone.'

'It could be worse. It could be, "He was a mane oul' whore."'

Nancy looks down at her glass. 'This is a strong mixture; I'd be afraid to drink it. I'm driving, you know.'

'Oh you'll be alright, you'll be alright,' Ned assures her.'

Nicky raises his glass in toast. 'Well, here's to our good health! And may we be in Heaven before the divil knows we're dead.'

Ned says, 'Good-luck.'

Nancy says 'Cheers' as she gingerly sips her drink.

Breda suddenly inquires, 'Nancy, are you in a hurry home?'

'No, not in any mad rush. What would I be rushing home to?'

'I'll tell you what you'll do; leave the car in town and come home with me?'

'That's exactly what you'll do,' Nicky quickly agrees. 'You can relax then with an easy mind.'

'It sounds the right sensible thing to do,' Ned encourages.

'Maybe that's what I will do. I wouldn't chance it. The guards around here are deadly. There are plenty of people I can get a lift in from in the morning.'

'That's the spirit,' Nicky declares. 'The Man who made time made plenty of it.'

'That's settled then?' Ned says.

'You wouldn't want to get caught anyhow. Jasus, you'd be lost without the old car. I know I chance it lots of times – the same as Ned there. It's not worth it though. You know something, if I had to do a driving test to get my insurance back, I wouldn't have a hope in hell.'

Ned nods in agreement. 'Not many like us would.'

'What kind of farming do you do, Nicky?' Breda asks.

'I'm a bully-beef man.' He indicates Ned. 'He's a single suckler.'

Nancy seems amused. 'A single suckler!'

Nicky continues, 'What difference anyhow; this oul' farmin' game is bet. No money in it anymore.'

'That's the truth,' Ned nods his head again in agreement. 'The beet is gone now and who knows what'll go next.'

'Sure the farmers are always complaining,' Nancy says. 'I'd say now, neither of you two is short of a few bob.'

'It's always a good tactic, a good policy, to have the poor mouth,' Nicky reminds her.

Ned, pint glass in hand, is reclining back on one of the high stools. Nicky is standing close by.

'The weather is never right. It's always either too wet or too dry,' Nancy smiles. 'Breda doesn't like to hear me say things like that either. Sure you don't?'

'I don't care.'

'The weather is a handy item for makin' conversation.' Nicky adds. 'That reminds me; hey, Ned, I met the young Brady wan yesterday. Like I was sayin' there, about the weather; just to be sayin' something I said, 'Tis cowld.' "If 'tis," she said, "pull your shirt down over it,"

Ned and Nicky laugh a little, but soon stop when they notice Nancy and Breda are not amused. Ned says, 'That would be her alright.'

'What do you think of that?' Nicky addresses Nancy. 'And she only after getting off the school bus.'

'You got your answer Nicky, didn't you. Maybe you shouldn't be watching young girls getting off the school bus.'

'Hold on now!' Nicky raises his arm. 'Hold your horses. That's a serious topic to bring up nowadays. The whole country is ripe with scandal. Things are gone to the dogs altogether. You have to be dead careful.'

'I'm only joking you.'

'I know that, I know that. But we're livin' in serious times. Fellas like us have to watch our every move. In all innocence, you do or say something, and you wouldn't know what way it would be taken up. It's as simple as this now: you just don't mix, meddle or make, with any of them youngsters. Not any more.'

'It's out of the question,' Ned confirms.

'Are things gone that bad?' Breda asks.

'You have to be fierce careful. Some of the things you'd hear about, girl, would make the hair stand on your head. Now Ned there and meself done a fair bit of travellin' in our time, didn't we?'

'God we did. Things were different back then – a lot different.'

'Maybe it was all kept behind closed doors,' Nancy suggests. 'Leopards don't change their spots, people don't change overnight.'

'Maybe. But we never came across anything…. anything peculiar though. Sure we didn't?'

'No, never,' Ned replies.

'We chased the ladies alright, but sure that's the way life goes.'

'As you can see, without much success,' Ned laments.

'Maybe you were too hard to please,' Nancy probes.

'No, no, far from it,' Ned replies.

'The chase, I suppose, was all part of the excitement,' Nicky explains. 'What I'm getting at is that 'twas all regular and above –board. Know what I mean?'

Breda stands up and points down the hallway. 'Is the….the…?'

Pointing, Ned directs, 'Down the hall – next to the gents.'

Nancy rises also. 'You can tell us about the women when we get back.' Picking up her handbag she follows Breda down the hallway.

Ned and Nicky are both on their feet now. Ned quickly asks, 'Well, what do you think?'

Enthusiastically, Nicky rubs his hands together with glee. 'Jasus, they're two right wans! We're in business boy. Breda is yours, right?'

'Yeh.' Ned appears a little subdued. 'Heh, listen, you don't think she's a bit....a bit quare, like?'

'What?'

'A bit.... A bit odd?'

'Are you mad, or something? What's wrong with you?'

Ned is seeking assurance. 'She's fine, isn't she?'

'She's fine, is right. Of course she is. See them shapely legs under her.' He puts his hand to his chest. 'And she have some pair of headlights. She's all there boy, all there.'

'That's what I was thinkin'.'

'What are you on about, then?'

'Nothin'. And listen to this: she have her own bit of ground – thirty one acres.'

'Christ, you're after landing on your two feet! You're elected.'

'You're not doing too bad for yourself either. Nancy looks the real business.' He clenches his fist and bends his arm. 'I'd say she's a right sporty wan.'

'She's a fine bird alright. I'll tell you wan thing, I'm not lavin' that quick now.'

'No wan's asking you.'

'Listen, what would you think? Would you say I have a chance?'

Ned nods the head and winks in the affirmative, 'I'd say she's interested alright. Definitely.'

'Would you? You're serious now? You're not coddin' me?'

'Out of the corner of me eye I saw her sizing you up. She'd suit you down to the ground. Remember though, what you said – about half the farm?'

'Don't mind that!' Nicky says dismissively.

'When you came in that door you never expected to find two of 'em?'

'No, be God. Surprised me alright. They hardly came together?'

'Nancy followed on. She's a smart bit of gear, I'd say.'

'Yeh, I'd say that.' Thumb indicating, 'I'd like to know what they're talkin' about right now. I wonder did we create an impression?'

Ned is non-committal. 'You never know what would be runnin' through a woman's head.'

'Your woman's sensible. No drink, huh?'

'She's dead set against it. It's a thorny subject with her. I'd better go aisy on it.'

'You'd better. Play your cards right now.' He gazes towards the hallway. 'Tell me this: why do women always follow each other down to the jacks? Do they hould on to each other when they bend down, or what?'

'They chat, put on the warpaint.'

'Hey, it's workin' out just right; I mean, the two of them and the two of us. It's a good job you put that thing on the paper.'

'Not so fast. Don't be counting your chickens.'

'Will we ask the two of 'em out together? Next Thursday night? What do you say?'

'We'll work around it. See what the lie of the land is first.'

''The only thing is, I'd say she have someone else. You'd know by her. She's bound to have.'

'No, she's there for you.'

'Is she? Are you sure?'

'I'm tellin' you. It's up to you now, to do your business.'

'I'll definitely chance me arm anyhow. You're getting on alright?'

'I think I am. But you wouldn't know. Hard to tell,'

'I hope no whore comes along now. We'll have a right old chat.'

'This place is always deserted. That's why….Whist!'

Nancy and Breda return.

'Pub Spy wouldn't want to visit that toilet,' Nancy says as she crosses to her seat,

'God above, it's in an awful state,' Breda confirms, as she too goes and sits down.

Nancy returns to the subject, 'You were on about all those women the two of you chased. I'm puzzled why you never settled down? I'm sure the women were throwing themselves at you.'

'Come on now, Nancy, you're coddin' us,' Ned says 'You're havin' us on.'

'I'm not. Nicky brought it up, didn't he?'

'Yeh, we travelled around alright. We did, I suppose, but in the heel of the hunt it didn't get us anywhere.'

'It was great fun though. Don't forget that,' Nicky emphasises. 'We had some great old times.'

'I'd say that,' Nancy says.

Nicky suddenly rubs his leg vigorously, going through the same motions as before. 'This bloody leg is giving me a touch of bother.' He hobbles about a bit. 'It's a thing of nothing.' He flicks the leg out a couple of times. 'That's better.' He straightens up. 'Oh yeh, we went all over the place. I remember the tail-end of the big dance band era. People travelled miles to hear those bands play.'

'Back then, we thought nothing of striking out for Killarney or Lisdoonvarna,' Ned relates.

'Remember the breaks we had in Lisdoon?' Nicky reminds Ned. 'Drinkin' and dancin' for days, hardly any sleep.'

Nancy probes, 'You were two hard men, I'd say. I'll bet you did some dancing and courting with the women up there?'

'Dancin' was the thing . You had to know your steps back then,' Ned explains. 'The Quick Step, The Slow Waltz, The Samba, The Foxtrot and my favourite, The Old Time Waltz.' He waltzes around a few times, giving his version of The Blue Danube. 'Die di di di dum, di dum, di dum'

He reaches down for Breda. 'Come on girl and I'll give you a twirl.'

Breda is unimpressed. 'You will not.' She pulls away his arm. 'It's bad enough you acting the clown without the two of us. And mind yourself now, or you'll fall over that chair.'

'It would take more drink than that girl, a lot more.' He staggers slightly.

'I'd say you're a good dancer, Nicky,' Nancy continues, 'or is your leg up to it anymore?'

'My leg is fine. There's nothin' wrong with me leg, don't worry about it.'

'It's not your leg I'd be worried about,' she laughs. 'Sorry, I'm only joking you.'

'You had to be fairly handy with the dancin' back in them days. The man was the driver like, and the woman expected you to know where you were going.'

'Did you ever come down our side – Dungarvan?'

'Of course we did – Clonea Strand,' Nicky informs her. 'Will I ever forget it. You'd hardly remember "The Sheep Breeders Dance" It was before your time. It was known as "The Ram Dance"'

'I heard of it. 'Twas famous. Did you hear of it, Breda?'

'I did. And I heard enough about it.'

'Everybody did. 'Twas an annual affair. We went there for years,' Ned says.

'Jasus there was some drink consumed on those nights. Never saw anything like it, before or since,' Nicky elaborates.

'A lot of rams around too, I'd say,' Nancy muses.

'Rams!' Nicky laughs loudly. 'A whole clatteren of 'em. Mad lookin' for ewes. Didn't matter if they were broken-mouthed, black-faced mountainy wans or not.'

'We were packed into them dancehalls like sardines,' Ned reminisces. 'Suds of sweat would be runnin' down the hollow of your spine. We didn't mind, though; we thought it was great. I suppose you look on the past through rose-tinted glasses. Isn't that what they say?'

'During all those years you must have had relationships with girls? Plenty of 'em,' Nancy queries.

'Oh we did, we did,' Ned responds.

'Several,' Nicky emphasises.

Ned shakes the head. 'They never seemed to last though, for some reason. Apart from wan girl – but we wont go into that. Maybe we just weren't cut out for sweet-talkin' the women.'

'We weren't that bad, mind,' Nicky corrects. 'We had some great laughs.'

'Maybe the girls didn't like the lifestyle they'd be

marrying into,' Nancy conjectures. 'Back twenty years or so ago, women were expected to work hard on farms. They worked inside and out, and got precious little for it. Isn't that right?'

'You have a point, I suppose,' Ned agrees. 'Some poor women were slaves: milkin' cows and feedin' pigs – and maybe rearing half a dozen children into the bargain.'

'Look at Breda: she's had a hard life – looking after an invalid and doing the work as well.'

'It was either that or sell the place,' Breda says.

Ned responds quickly, 'Oh God, you done the right thing in holdin' on to it. The money would trickle away, and then you'd be left with nothing. Mark my words, you done the right thing.'

'Anyway, it's a different story nowadays,' Nicky pontificates. 'The women don't have to put a hand outside the door.'

Ned and Nicky are drinking steadily. Ned mentions the obvious. 'They all have other jobs. They're independent.'

'Fair play to 'em,' Nancy says with conviction. 'About time they had their own money. I wouldn't dream of giving up my job if I married. Those days are gone forever.'

Nicky nods in agreement, 'You'd be right, dead right.'

Ned, looking away, in thought, says, 'You know, you might be right – about the women and the lifestyle. Never looked at it that way. I was wondering was there something wrong with us, or what.'

'And what about yourselves now?' Nicky asks. 'You're still fine lookin' women, but you're shovin' on a bit too – if you don't mind me saying so?' He raises his hand. 'I'm sorry now, I'm sorry. Maybe I shouldn't have said that.'

'It's alright. Where I'm concerned it's a long story and wouldn't interest you,' Nancy says. 'Anyway, why do men always assume that single girls have nothing on their minds but marriage? Maybe in my case I just don't like men, I've seen too much of 'em, I don't trust 'em. What do you make of that?' Nicky is looking at her, open-mouthed. 'What are you looking at? You think I'm a lesbian, is that it?'

'A what?... Oh yeh, I know what you're getting at. That never crossed my mind. God no.'

'If I were itself it would be my own business.'

'Somebody asked wan time, were we that way inclined,' Ned announces. 'The same man himself was, I believe.' He indicates Nicky, with a nod of the head. 'Imagine him an' me! Christ, that would bate all out.'

'I'd say you'd be the most unlikely pair in the whole world,' Nancy proclaims.

'Strange thoughts run in people's minds,' Ned adds. 'We travelled around together so much, maybe.'

Breda looks from one to the other. 'Some people would say anything.'

Nicky, in a serious tone of voice asks, 'Nancy, did it ever enter your head that maybe it might be nice to settle down, if the right man came along?'

'If the right man came along?... I think at this stage you could safely say marriage is out of the equation.'

'It wouldn't be if I was in the runnin'.'

Nancy looks over, in amazement, 'What are you saying?'

Nicky impulsively blurts out, 'Honest to God! I'd marry you in the mornin', if you'd have me.'

'What!' Glancing at Breda, Nancy appears as if she doesn't know whether to laugh or to cry.

A rustling sound in the hallway announces the arrival of Foxy and Trish. Nicky is unaware.

'That's the truth,' Nicky says with fervour.

Foxy and Trish make their grand entrance. On seeing them, with exasperation, Nicky gasps, "Fuck!"

Foxy's countenance lights up when he observes the company. 'Christ Trish!' he exclaims, 'will you just look at who's here; the two boys – Mick Collins and The Long Fella.'

Chapter Twelve

Long Night's Journey Into Day

Foxy has bought two large bottles of cider. Trish has gone and sat by a table to oneside, a puzzled frown on her face at the cool reception. Breda and Nancy appear gob-smacked by the new arrivals. Nicky, especially, is none too pleased. Foxy crosses with a bottle and glass to Trish.

Passing Nicky, he says, 'And how are you, Nicky?'

'I'm alright,' Nicky grunts,

'You don't sound alright.'

'What's it to you? I'm fine.'

Trish says, 'Thanks.' Foxy doesn't use a glass.

'I didn't expect to see you,' Ned remarks.

'I know you didn't. And you don't look too happy about it. Aren't you goin' to introduce me to your friends?'

With undisguised reluctance Ned says, 'Breda and Nancy, meet Foxy.' He points, 'and that's Trish over there.'

Breda and Nancy say, 'Hello.'

Trish says, 'How are you.'

Foxy adds, 'At least it's nice to meet two polite people.'

Ned says, 'What the hell brings you in here, Foxy? I thought a place like this would be too quiet for you.'

This place is a kip,' Foxy declares, placing the guitar on

one of the tables. 'There's more life in a seven day old corpse. I'll tell you what brings me in; I meet a fella here at the weekends and he sells me a bit of weed. Just on the off-chance, I thought I'd look in. That satisfy you?'

'Drugs!' Nancy says, with distain. 'What next?'

'What's wrong with you? It's only a smoke, that's all.'

'That's what they all say.'

With a tone of solemn warning Breda adds, 'Next thing you'll be sticking needles in your arm.'

'No way,' Foxy declares emphatically. 'Christ, I'm not a fool. Old McTaggart outside don't know what goes on in here; in this den of iniquity.' With a dismissive wave of the hand he continues. 'He don't give a damn either, he have his money made.' He stands over Breda and Nancy. 'Breda and Nancy, two handy names to remember. Ned, you asked me what I was doing here; I can see what you two are doing – out on a big double date.'

'We've met a couple of friends for a chat,' Ned replies. 'That's all there's to it.'

'Oh-hoh, I've heard that one before. And sure what would be wrong with it? A sign of health. But then, you two fellows are known far and wide.' He places his hand on Breda's shoulder. 'Did you ever hear of Shergar? Did you?'

Breda obviously did. 'What about him?'

'He had a short enough life. Before he died they say he covered a lot of mares. But I'll tell you this much,

Shergar couldn't hold a candle to the amount of women these two boys covered.'

Ned and Nicky bristle with indignation.

'Foxy, you bastard, what are you sayin'',' Nicky barks.

'Holy Christ, a slap in the mouth you need!' Ned adds. He has his fist raised as if he is about to oblige. Foxy, grinning, warily backs away, on the defensive.

Nicky blusters, 'Comin' in here with your – your – '

'Lies and filth.'

Breda is appalled. She rises, addressing Nancy, 'Will we go?'

Nancy is also on her feet. 'I think we'd better.'

Ned attempts to pacify them. 'No, don't go! Hold on, hold on. Don't mind him; don't mind that idiot.'

Nicky is struggling to contain himself. 'That —that clown.'

'I'm only joking,' Foxy laughs. 'What's wrong with ye? Don't be so touchy.'

'That's not joking,' Ned rasps.

'Bloody tipper. Don't know where they got you from,' Nicky mumbles.

'Can't you take a joke? Have you any sense of humour?' He holds his hands wide. 'Ladies, you were hardly going to walk out on us, were you? Sure Nicky there and myself are related. We're all the wan. You'd hardly insult the present company by walking out?'

Breda and Nancy sit back down.

'If we're related 'tis far out,' Nicky stresses. 'The rest of the family might be okay, but I don't know where they dropped you from.'

'The black sheep, am I? Anyway, take it easy, don't be losin' the run of yourselves. Enjoy yourselves, that's the thing. That's the only thing that matters in the long run. You're only passing through this old world once, so make the most of it.'

Ned lounges back on one of the high stools, still discomfited looking. 'There's jokin' and jokin' in it.'

Trish is sitting demurely, sipping her cider, legs spread out, white thighs exposed.

'And what part are you ladies from?' Foxy inquires.

'Near Dungarvan,' Breda replies.

'Dungarvan,' Foxy repeats. 'So you're Waterford then. I'll tell you this much; we're goin' to win the All Ireland; we're goin' to bate ye; we'll bate Tipperary, Kilkenny, the whole fuckin' lot! Up the Rebels!' He punches the the air with his fist. 'Up the Rebels!' He looks over towards Trish. 'Trish, are you gone asleep, or what?'

'Foxy, I'm tired. Do you know what time we went to bed last night? 'Twas after four o'clock.'

Foxy spots Nicky casting sly glances at Trish's naked cleavage. 'Nicky, what do you think of her?' Putting his hands under Trish's armpits he helps her to her feet. 'Look at that body. Don't you think she's a fair bird? She have it all in the right places. If she was a racehorse

Trish is stopped short in her tracks. 'I hope that don't mean what I'm thinkin' it might mean. I don't like smartalicky talk.'

'What are you on about,?' Nancy retorts, with feigned innocence.

'You know well. I can give as good as I get, so be careful.' Foxy returns. Trish grabs hold of Ned's right hand and holds it out. 'Will you look at the size of his hands; you could mix concrete with them.'

Ned pulls his hand away. 'Don't annoy me now.'

'Foxy, give us a song. I told them you write funny songs, but I don't think they believe me.'

Foxy looks about. 'Maybe that's what I'll do. Would you like to hear one of my compositions?' Trish slumps back into her chair. Foxy proceeds to take the guitar out of the case. 'I wrote this song when I was off the beer.'

'When did that miracle happen,?' Ned cynically inquires.

'Miracle is right,' Nicky snorts.

'I got into a bit of bother with the law, you see, and the ould judge put me on probation. One of the conditions was that I stay away from the booze. I stuck it for a couple of weeks. A new life, I thought; a new beginning. But, alas, I thought wrong…. I haven't arranged this right yet, so maybe it sounds a bit off-key. I'll just use the old guitar as an accompaniment.' He points at Ned. 'I could have called this "Ned" after you.'

'Could you now.'

'But I didn't, It's called "Goodbye to the Beer." Here

goes then.' He commences to sing and to strum the guitar.

'When you're off the beer, your old mind it is clear,
You'll have no regrets the next morning,
You'll remember where you've been, and who you have seen,
You'll go to work whistling a tune,
You're head feels so good, no lump-hammer whacking your brain,
No bad hangovers, those days are all over,
You've kissed goodbye to the beer,
Yes, you've kissed goodbye to the beer.

But the other night it did happen and look at the state you're in now,
You're poor girlfriend had enough, she ran home to her mother in tears,
You got in a fight, you thought you could never be beaten,
But the man from the hill, with a fist that could kill,
Sent you crashing right over the table,
You pulled yourself up as the police car arrived,
And straight away you were struck by a baton.
Just look at you now, with your eyes black and blue,
Your nose is all flat, and part of your left ear is missing,
You have cuts to your chin, so that you can't even grin,
A large gap where your front teeth were once flashing.

But Ned you've seen the light, you've finally got bright,
This world it was made for clean livin',
Your girlfriend and mine, we'll have a good time,
We'll go for a spin on our bikes,
We'll be laughin' an' kissin',and the sun will be shining,

So who gives a damn anyhow.
You know, your nose and your ear wont look all that bad,
And your new front teeth will look as good as your own,
No more bad hangovers, those days are all over,
You've kissed goodbye to the beer,
Yes, you've kissed goodbye to the beer.'

He finishes with a flourish on the guitar and holds out his hands, saying, 'Well, what do you think?' There is a subdued response.

'There you are now,' Trish says. 'You know you could have called it "Ned," after himself there. There's a kind of similarity about it.'

'What are you sayin'!' Ned snaps.

Foxy looks around. 'I hear no clappin', no applause.?'

'You wouldn't win the Eurovision with that yoke anyhow,' Nicky declares.

'A pity you didn't stay off the beer,' Ned remarks.

'The words are good. I'd agree with the words,' Breda's verdict.

Nancy says, 'It seems you're a man of many talents.'

'What did I tell you? I told you he could do it.'

Foxy looks around. 'Anybody else for a song?... No one?... None of you? Hey Ned, how about "The Banks?"'

'I think we've enough singin' for tonight,' Nicky says with finality.

Foxy stands directly in front of Breda and Nancy and commences to sing,

'Dungarvan my home town,
I love best of all,
Dear old faces and places,
Sure oft I recall,
In my heart I keep wishing,
Some day I will be,
Back again in Dungarvan,
My home by the sea.

Nancy, how about it? Come on.'

'No thanks.' She is adamant.

'That's it then?... None of ye?.... You're no damn good.' Foxy proceeds to put the guitar back in the case. 'You're all dead wires – the whole bloody lot of ye.'

'I'll give you a song,' Trish volunteers.

'Nourishment I want, not punishment', Foxy retorts.

'There's thanks for you'.

'Why don't you go up to Denby's?' Ned suggests. 'There's music up there most nights.'

'Trying to get rid of us, are you? Don't worry, we'll be gone soon.'

'I could do with an early night,' Trish urges. 'You hear me?'

'Yeh, yeh. Just take it easy.' He places his hand on Nancy's shoulder. 'Do you know what people always called their two families? – "The Micks and The Devs."'

Ned jumps in, 'Families have nicknames. Everywan knows that.'

Foxy is on a roll. 'It goes all the way back to the Civil

116

War: Ned's family, you see, were ferocious Michael Collins' supporters, while Nicky's were Devs' to the backbone. Christ, there used be murder between 'em. They couldn't stand each other. They hated each other's guts.'

Nicky is quickly on the defensive, 'We didn't hate each other. What the hell are you talkin' about?'

Ned joins in, 'Not like that. Hate, now, hate, that's a strong word in any man's language.'

Foxy is enjoying himself, 'They had fist-fights in pubs, everywhere. Up Dev! Come on Mick!'

'Things were hot back in those days,' Ned explains to Nancy and Breda.

Nicky nods in agreement, 'That's the way it was.'

'Later on, Ned's crowd marched with the Blueshirts.' Foxy now flicks the lapel of Ned's shirt.

'Take your paw off me.'

'See, he's still wearing the old blue shirt. General Owen O'Duffy, boy! I know me history.' He stands to attention. As Ned reaches for his pint of Guinness he gets a slap between the shoulders that almost sends him sprawling. 'Salute your senior officer!'

With the glass held in one hand Ned makes a swipe at Foxy who easily avoids him. He tries again. 'You're goin' too far! I've had enough –' Aware of the female company he controls himself and calms down.

Nancy and Breda look towards each other and appear on the brink of leaving again.

Foxy dances about. 'Heh, lighten up! We're only havin' a bit of fun. Enjoy life.'

'Your kind of fun. The fun of the tipper.'

'Forget about all that old stuff from the past,' Nicky says. 'Openin' up old wounds is bad news. We're gone beyond all that, thank God; we're livin' in different times.'

'Foxy, you're only draggin' this up now to see can you get us two goin', Ned implies. 'You want a bit of a laugh, don't you?'

'Not at all; everyone knows about ye.'

Ned addresses Breda and Nancy directly, 'He's right. What he said about us is the truth. That's the way our families were, back then.'

'Not anymore, I hope?' Nancy quizzes.

'You can be certain sure of it.' Nicky is again motivated. 'Years ago, Ned and myself signed our own treaty. Isn't that right?'

'Dead right.'

'Put it there,' Nicky says. They clasp hands as if to re-affirm their pact. ''Twas long ago we realized we were nothing but two hard-boiled idiots; two village pump politicians; two clowns, nothing more.'

Foxy grins, 'So you saw the light?'

'We were clowns alright,' Ned agrees. 'At election time we'd go around with our roof-racks and ladders, tearin' down the other party's posters and stickin' up our own. Stupid ould foolish things like that.'

'Tryin' to get certain people to vote at two different polling booths. You know, the usual,' Nicky adds. 'That we were feckin' idiots, is the truth.' He gets animated now as he reminisces. 'And what did we get out of it? Answer me that? Vote Fianna Fail! Vote Fine Gael!' Christ almighty!'

Ned has become equally agitated. 'Years ago, when I asked 'em, did Fine Gael licence my bull? They did like hell!' He taps Nicky on the shoulder. 'Did Fianna Fail tar your boreen? Well, did Fianna Fail tar your boreen? They did in my arse!'

Nicky is resolute. 'I wouldn't cross the road for any of that crowd.'

Ned derides, 'Drawing big salaries above in Dail Eireann, an' laughin' at you. You don't have to tell me. Politicians how are yah!'

Nancy, surprisingly, joins in, 'You only see 'em when the election comes round.'

'Exactly,' Nicky agrees.

Foxy crosses to go down the hallway, clenched fist raised in the air again, shouting en-route, 'Up Dev! Up the Blueshirts! Woh!'

'Anyway, I believe the Civil War was harmless in our parish; nobody killed or injured, thank God,' Nicky says, head bowed in thought.

'Apart from Sniper McCarthy,' Ned reminds him. 'Hiding up an ivy tree, waiting for the Free State Army to show; when he saw 'em comin' he got such a fright he fell off the tree and broke his leg.'

'He got a pension out of that,' Nicky states.

'Oh he did, and a medal.'

Nicky turns to Trish and points down the hall. 'Is there something wrong with his kidneys – or what?'

Trish stands up and moves across. 'He's just gone down to the toilet to smoke a bit of grass; gone for a few drags.'

Breda appears puzzled. 'What? Smoke grass? Grass?

Trish is now standing centre. 'Foxy is me partner, you know that?'

'I kind of figured that,' Nancy responds.

Trish surveys the company. 'Are you all connected some way?... Going out together, maybe?'

'We're just friends, out for a quiet drink, that's all,' Nancy says.

Trish doesn't appear too convinced. 'Just wondering.... You found a quiet spot alright; this place is as dead as a dodo. ... I've been going out with Foxy, on and off, since I was sixteen – and that wasn't yesterday or the day before.'

Nancy inquires, 'Why is he called "Foxy"? Was his hair—?'

'Nothing to do with his hair. I'll tell you why,' Trish explains, 'when he was about eighteen he used to go after the foxes, in the night-time, with a rifle. I used be with him. My job was to carry this big bloody battery – and a torch, that would blind you at two hundred yards. 'Twas deadly. I'd make a noise like a wounded rabbit.'....She demonstrates, by blowing through her fingers, making a plaintive sound, similar to a wounded small animal. 'Like that. The fox would come to investigate, I'd dazzle him, and Foxy would plug him. He had some shot. We travelled round in a battered ould Ford van; we'd throw the dead foxes in the back. Jasus, there was some smell off that van – and off our clothes.'

Nancy makes a face, 'I could imagine!'

'I remember that time alright,' Nicky states. 'The Department brought out that scheme.'

'The sheep men were behind it.'

'That's right.'

'He was a form of bounty hunter, then,' Nancy comments.

'We had to cut the tongues out of the foxes; you got paid for 'em at the guards' barracks...'Twas a bit messy alright.'

Breda grimaces,' Oh God.'

'You'd grow accustomed to anything, you know that. I'll tell you wan thing, you couldn't get the basterin' smell off yourself. When you'd go into the pub afterwards, you'd notice people lookin' around, wonderin' what the pong was. Then, when you'd go up to the chipper, your man behind the counter would stick his nose in the air, sniffin' like an oul' jackass, thinkin' maybe his fish was gone rotten again. Christ, it used be gas.' She smiles at the memory. 'I often have to laugh when I think back to those times. Anyway, that's how the name stuck. He's known by nothin' else...' Her gaze lingers on Nancy.

'Hey, don't forget about that job now. Put a word in for me.'

'No, I wont forget. What does Foxy work at?'

'He's on the buildings. Oh, and he draws the dole as well. That's why he have to travel a good bit away from home. He wouldn't want to be spotted workin' – know what I mean? You'll keep that to yourselves now, wont you? I do a bit of house-cleanin' myself, around the town. People trust me in their homes. I'd do any kind of work, to tell you the truth. I hate bein' idle. Foxy have no hold on money though, that's the worst part of it. Burns a hole in his pocket. What he loses on the horses is nobody's business. Sometimes I feel like wringin' his scrawny neck.'

'I don't know where they got him in the litter,' Ned concludes.

Foxy returns. He crosses, puts his hand on Nicky's shoulder and starts to sing,
'Oh I threw it out to sea,
But it floated back to me,
That old red flannel drawers that Maggie wore.
Isn't it great to be alive.' He points off to the distance. 'Christ, there are men up there in that cemetery who'd love to be here with us tonight. Feck 'em all boy! Feck 'em all! You only get the wan chance, so make the most of it.' He does a bit of shadow-boxing, including the Muhammid Ali shuffle. 'Come on Nicky, we'll have a bit of a scrap. You said I badly need a good clatter in the mouth.'

'If you're not careful that's what you'll get.'

'Heh, remember the old Volkswagen Beetle you had wan time? She was some car. Brammh! Brammh! Brammh! Remember the roar of the engine? You'd swear you were drivin' a German Tiger Tank. I got a spin from you wan day and Christ, I'll never forget it: the exhaust pipe was hangin' off, and when you'd look down you'd see the road in spots. Me heart was in me mouth. I was certain I was goin' to go through the floor.'

'Pity you didn't.'

'If you brought that yoke to the test centre today you'd be arrested.'

'The best car I ever had. Pity they don't make 'em anymore.'

As usual, Ned agrees. ''Twas a great car.'

'And Christ Ned, you have another beauty – the old Bluebird.'

'That car passed her test, so shut your mouth.'

'There's hopes for us all then.' He bends down and speaks in a confidential manner to Breda and Nancy. 'You know, them two boys travelled Munster in that Bluebird. That's what the people say. If that old jalopy could talk what a story she'd tell. All the courtin' that was done in the back of that passion wagon.'

Ned has become incensed again. 'Mind yourself now, Foxy, I'm warnin' yah! Don't be pushin' your luck.'

Foxy ignores him. 'All the women who experienced ecstasy in the back of that Bluebird.'

Trish is getting impatient. 'You'll annoy people Foxy, will

you shut up. They only came in for a quiet drink.' She stands up. 'Come on, we'll be off. Come on.'

'Hold your horses. What's the mad hurry? We'll have wan more drink for the road. Then we'll be off.'

'Mind your big mouth then. I have enough drink, anyhow.'

'We'll all have something,' Foxy says, with a magnanimous gesture. 'On me, come on.'

'Stay the way you are, for God's sake,' Nicky implores.

'Without conviction Ned says, 'We've had enough of it.'

'Whist! Be quiet an' drink up! What is it?'

'I've enough, anyhow; no more for me,' Nancy declares.

'Wan more wont kill you. The same again? We'll all have the same again.' Breda shakes her head. Foxy bangs on the serving hatch.

Chapter Thirteen

Lifestyle and High Finance

A short period of time has elapsed. Trish is stretched back, displaying even more of her natural attributes than previous. Though trying to be attentive to Nancy, Nicky is still distracted by the image.

'I'm flogged tired tonight,' Trish exclaims. 'All this is madness.'

Breda half rises, 'It's moving on; maybe we should be going.'

'Hold on, sure 'tis early yet. Finish your drinks. Drink up. Heh Nicky, you've nearly a full pint there; never let it be said you left the fine stuff behind you.'

'Don't be too long then, and give us a bit of peace for the love of God,' Ned implores.

Foxy points to the general bar area. 'You know, that wan he have workin' for him wouldn't entice you in to this joint. She's as sour as a crab-apple. Throw the old drink at you. You'd think you were getting it for nothing.'

'And the money don't fall off the trees,' Ned expounds.

Foxy displays a fresh alertness. 'Money! Now there's a subject worth talkin' about. Ned, how much are you makin' at home on the old ranch?'

'What?' Ned is somewhat taken aback.

'How much money? Per annum?'

'For feck sake!' Ned gulps... 'That's a private matter....Christ, you don't go around ...'

'All that money you're getting' from Brussels. Oh come on, I'm sure the ladies would like to know.'

Breda intercedes. 'That's his own business.'

'It certainly is,' Nancy, likewise, concurs.

Foxy cajoles, 'A man of your means. An important man. Come on?'

'What am I making...?' Ned is contemplating, thinking that maybe this is an opportunity to impress.

'Yeh...Why all the secrecy? What's the big deal about?'

Ned rubs his chin, perplexed, unsure. He decides. 'I suppose I'm makin' the bones of fifteen thousand a year.'

'Fifteen thousand!' Foxy repeats in a loud voice.

Ned looks around, smiling, pretty pleased with himself. 'You heard me. Fifteen thousand – maybe a little more.'

'That's only piss money.'

Ned's face slumps. 'What are you sayin'?'

Foxy adds with derision, 'A good waiter in a restaurant would make that on tips. And how much are you earnin' Nicky, me oul' flower?'

Nicky glances towards Nancy. 'Me? A year?.... Oh, I'd say about fifty grand.'

Foxy acts incredulous. 'What are you sayin? You're makin' fifty and your farm is smaller than Ned's. You must be sellin' opium. Feckin' poppies you must be growing up on that hill.' Grinning, he points his finger. 'Oh I know what it is; he's trying to impress someone. Isn't that it, Nicky?'

'Because you're called Foxy you think you're a smart bastard, don't you? Well that's where you're wrong.'

'Hey, listen, I was hunting rabbits up your way on Sunday. You have a few miserable, hungry cows above in that barn. Christ, they are nearly transparent; you could almost see through 'em.'

Nicky, as Foxy intended, is getting riled again. 'Feck all you know about 'em.'

'When wan of 'em went to bawl she had to lean against the wall.'

Nicky advances on Foxy. 'Feck you now, Foxy. You're goin' on an' on, getting on my nerves —'

Breda quickly rises, 'Don't start a row. Please take it easy. Maybe we should –'

Reassuringly— but still keeping a wary eye on Nicky – Foxy says, 'Don't worry, there'll be no row. We know each other too well, don't we? A bit of banter is what we're havin'. Sure we're related.'

'As I said before, it's way out – and it's worse luck.'

'You're always getting into arguments and rows,' Trish interrupts. 'I think I'll make my own way home.'

'Take it easy, don't be rushing me. Just relax, will you.' She sits back down. 'Now if Ned is makin' fifteen you're probably on fourteen.'

'It's none of your feckin' business. I can get by. Ned or

myself have no great expense.'

'You're right there' Ned agrees. 'That's the thing, you see'

Nicky moves his finger across his throat, 'I'm not up to here in hock, smothered in debts and mortgages. I might be drivin' a banger, but at least I own it. I could be drivin' around in wan of them big four-wheel-drive jeeps, but 'tis the Bank of Ireland who'd own it. Feck that for a caper.'

'People are livin' above their means,' Ned states with conviction. 'Wait'll the bubble bursts. There'll be a big crash wan of those days. Mark my words.'

Foxy disagrees. 'That's it you see, that's more of it. You have the wrong attitude altogether. If everybody thought like you nothing would happen. Things are flyin'. Things were never better. Houses are springin' up like mushrooms all over the place. It's jumpin' on the tiger's back you should be – instead of draggin' out of his tail.'

'Wait'll you see. You'll be sayin' yet, "Ned was right."'

'Doom and gloom!' Foxy mutters. 'Christ! Fifteen grand a year. Living in poverty on the side of a hill. In this day and age. Do you know how much I'm earning? Nicky, have a guess.'

'I don't give a tinker's curse what you're earnin'.'

'No wan gives a damn.'

'I'm knockin' down over a thousand a week, handy. Add in the Christmas bonus, the overtime; I suppose I'd be on over fifty-five thousand a year. Then I top that up with the dole. The funny thing is, I don't know where the hell it all goes to. That's the thing. That's the fuckin' mystery.'

'The horses, the booze,' Trish says balefully.

'Shut up!'

'Other things too. Oh you know well.'

'Do you hear her?'

'Do you ever stop talking,? Nancy asks.

'No,' he replies.

'I was thinking that.'

Nicky has another bout of "dead leg syndrome." 'Blast and feck this leg,' he mumbles.

Trish has a sudden brainwave, 'Maybe if Nicky and Ned bought two shovels and went to work –'

Foxy quickly intervenes, 'On the buildings! Them two! They wouldn't be able for it.' He points, 'With that leg, up on a ladder. What kind of fool would hire them two?'

Ned jumps in, 'The same kind of fool who hired you, maybe.'

'You'd be too lazy. You wouldn't get your arses out of bed in the morning.'

'That's more of it.'

'We'd be round pegs in square holes,' Ned states. 'We'll stick with what we know.'

'Life is too cushy for you. What do you do every day, Nicky? Get up and have the boiled egg, go out, hop up on the old Massey Ferguson and count the few hungry cattle; come in for the ten o'clock tay, then throw yourself down on the sofa and dream about that woman from Thailand.'

'Little you know boy, little you know,' Ned says with a measure of disgust. 'You're up in the clouds, you haven't a clue.'

Looking about, Nicky declares, 'Wouldn't that kind of ignorant talk annoy you?'

'Did you see her lately?'

Nicky replies to this query with a curt, 'No!'

Nancy is curious. 'What woman from Thailand?'

'This ould fella – livin' out near them two – disappeared for a month or so. No sign of him. Everywan thought the poor ould devil was after jumpin' off the Cliffs of Moher, or something. The parish was preparing for a funeral when suddenly he arrived home with this gorgeous woman from Thailand. The whole place was stunned, amazed.'

'That's a good wan alright,' Nancy smiles. 'some man.'

'She walks like this.' He demonstrates, walking up and down, swaying his hips. 'And she have a smile that would melt a stone. If she smiled at Ned there he'd go weak at the knees. All the women are jealous of her – and all the men love her.'

'Including yourself, I suppose,' Trish implies. 'Maybe that's what takes you out that way so often.'

'Nicky, aren't I right about her?'

Nicky gestures distainfully, 'Ah, don't be coddin' me.'

'It's a strange world. She seems to be mad about him. It's something I can't understand. What is it about women? Tell me that.'

Nancy puts her hand to her forehead. 'I feel a bit queasy after drinking that stuff.'

Breda is immediately concerned. 'Are you alright?'

'What's wrong?, Nicky inquires anxiously.

'Nothing.'

Breda moves across. 'Are you sure?'

'I'm alright, it'll wear off.'

'Don't touch any more of that,' Breda advises.

'Don't worry, I wont. It's alright, I'm okay.'

Foxy looks about. 'Well, anyhow, Dungarvan is nearer than Thailand. What's the story here? Who's with who? I'd say the way Ned is sniffin' around Breda that pairs you off. Ned and Breda, and Nancy and Nicky. A double wedding, huh?'

Nancy glares at him. 'That attitude irritates me. Straight away you're jumping to conclusions; just because the four of us are talking here we must be tied up some way. There's such a thing as platonic friendship.'

'What would be wrong with it?'

Breda changes the subject. 'What you were saying, about the work on a small farm; it's not that simple. It's hard enough to make ends meet. You can be certain sure of it.'

Foxy turns to her. 'How do you know?'

Ned interjects, 'Because she lives on wan, and works on it.'

'You're at home with your father then?'

'He's dead. I'm on my own.'

Foxy registers surprise. 'On your own?'

Ned again intercedes, 'Are you deaf?'

'Livin' on your own? In a farmhouse, on your own?'

'Yes.'

'Nowadays, in the country? That's dangerous, with the climate that's in it. I'm telling you.'

'It wouldn't be me,' Trish shakes her head, 'I wouldn't be happy in wan of them big lonely houses in the daytime – let alone the night.'

'It's hard every way;' Breda says. Ned glances at her, fearful that she might be off on another tirade like before. His fears are groundless however, and she continues. 'you can't get a person to give you a hand for love nor money. Everybody is working in town. I'd be lost only that Nancy helps out in the evenings and at the weekends.'

'I like working with animals. I think I prefer animals to human beings.'

Nicky tilts the head, 'What? What did you say?'

'Never mind,' Nancy blithely says. 'Anyway, the exercise does me good. It's great therapy. I'd need to get off a few pounds as well.'

Trish feels her waist. 'Like us all. It's easier said than done though. All them oul' diets are useless, if you ask me.'

Foxy stands, looking down at Breda. 'Why don't you team up with Ned there?. That would solve your problem.'

Ned doesn't appear to know how to react. 'Do you hear him,' he guffaws, mirthlessly.

'You'd solve the world's problems, wouldn't you?' Nancy sniggers.

'Yourself and Nicky would be well matched too.'

'All neatly packaged, no bother.'

He holds out his two upturned hands. 'What would be wrong with it? To be honest about it none of you could be called a spring-chicken. Maybe you have a man in your life already, Nancy, have you?'

'Shut up,' Breda hastily exclaims.

'You're right!' Nancy suddenly becomes overwrought. 'I know I'm no spring-chicken. I know that. That other bastard wasted my best years.'

Breda now pleads, 'I keep telling you, put him out of your mind. You've got to.'

Ned looks a little confused. 'What's wrong? What is it?...What's up?.'

'There's nothing wrong,' Breda admonishes him.

'If there's something on your chest girl get rid of it.' Trish says.

'Are you alright? The old drink, maybe,' Nicky theorizes.

'Shut up you! It's not the drink. Shit! What about it. Everybody knows about it anyway: I was courting this bastard for years; we were engaged and he jilted me. That's what's wrong.'

Trish exhales loudly, 'Christ!... that's... that's tough, that's hard.'

'Everybody thought we'd be married. It's all a fuckin' nightmare.'

'Sorry to hear that now,' Ned says uncomfortably.

Nicky agrees, solemnly nodding his head, 'Yeh, same here.' In fact, Nicky is not one bit sorry as he feels he might now be in with a fighting chance.

'You have no idea what it's like, how it feels.'

'I think I have,' Ned says.

Foxy throws him a quick glance, 'Who! You?'

'All the dreams and plans I had,' Nancy laments bitterly. 'I could think of no one but him. I should have known! It was all dragged out so long. I was just used, nothing more. Discarded then, like a piece of dirt off his boot... People telling me how sorry they were the romance broke up. I have to listen to that every day. Someone brings it up the whole time....God!'

'People can be cruel without knowing it, can't they?' Trish says.

'Look at it this way,' Foxy consoles, 'you're lucky to be rid of the fecker.'

'Went off and married a girl years younger than himself. He wanted children, that's what it was…. He was going out with her the same time as he was meeting me. Twelve years! He ruined my life.'

'Plenty of fish in the sea.' Foxy puts his hand on Nicky's shoulder. 'This is the fish for you.'

Nancy rises. 'I feel half sick now. I don't know what way I am.'

Breda puts her arm around her. 'Take it easy.'
Trish crosses. 'Are you alright? Is your stomach upset?'

'That mixture you had; maybe it was too much for you,' Nicky surmises.

Nancy blurts out, 'He's some bastard, that's what he is.'

'Come on out in the hall,' Trish urges. 'We'll open the street door and get a breath of fresh air. You'll be alright. Take it easy.'

'Splash some cold water up on your face,' Breda suggests. 'It'll freshen you.'

Nancy exclaims with rancour, as she is linked out, 'That's why I prefer dogs and animals to men; an old dog will wag his tail and stand by you the whole time; he'll never let you down, never leave you on the lurch.' They exit, down the hallway.

Nicky, Ned and Foxy look from one to the other. Foxy speaks first, 'What do you make of that?'

Ned seeks confirmation, 'She didn't drink too much, did she?'

'She only had a couple. The wine mixed in it mightn't

be the best,' Nicky feels.

'It's a stronger mix than you'd think, I'd say,' Foxy states.

'She's not under the weather,' Ned decides. 'More on the sick side. Jasus, she's fierce upset over what happened.'

Nicky concurs, 'Hard to blame her. That's a fair blow to get. She's in a state alright.'

'You have your work cut out, Nicky boy,' Foxy grins. 'When a bird prefers a dog to a man, you're in trouble.'

Nicky suddenly and speedily catches Foxy by the collar of the shirt and proceeds to "chuck" him about. 'You're not doin' us any good, are you? Takin' the piss out of us all night.'

Foxy is unperturbed, laughing, 'Good man Nicky! There's life in the old dog yet.' He receives a few hefty swings, almost lifting him off the floor. 'Hey, watch it! Cut it out!'

Ned guards the table containing the drink. 'Be careful! Mind the drink.'

Chapter Fourteen

The Law and Nicky Daly

Barry Moloney was the name of the Garda Siochana that Nicky almost bumped into as he emerged from The Deli restaurant. Barry was conscious of his training at Templemore, where it was instilled into all trainee gardai to be ever vigilant, and always, when stationed in a small town, to keep an eye out for strange faces. On that basis, referring to this unexpected encounter with Nicky, Garda Moloney said to himself, 'I didn't see that old buzzard around before.' This was his fourth week stationed in Youghal.

Back at the station, Sergeant Bulley expressed himself as being well pleased with this new arrival to the force. 'He was cut from the same cloth as himself,' Sergeant Bulley concluded. Being cut from "the same cloth" meant you took no prisoners. With Sergeant Bulley, black was black, white was white, and there was no grey area in between. Aged fifty-three, he could be classified as extremely dour and strict, belonging to the old school of thought. He held strong views from which he rarely deviated. He detested alcoholic drink in any form, and firmly believed that ninety-nine per cent of all the trouble in the country emanated from the pub – "the source of all evil" – as he called it. "Didn't most of the serious road accidents happen late at night, when people – mostly young people — took a chance, and drove when they were tanked up with alcohol. How many fights and murders happen when the pubs close?," he often asked. Other drugs — which were now spreading rapidly all over the country — were also fast becoming the bane of his life. The first advice he gave each morning, to any member of the force under his command was, 'Show no mercy to grug-pushers.' Those people he referred to as "the scum of the earth."

Another social problem which rankled deeply with Jim Bulley was the decline in moral standards throughout the land. He was an orthodox religious believer, and a rigid conservative in his thinking. He found it hard to come to terms with the way times had changed, in particular the laize-fare attitude to all things sexual. He longed for a return to the old ways, where the dignity of women was truly respected. To his way of thinking, anything to do with pornography was wicked in the extreme — and surely inspired by the devil. The purveyors of such evil were, he felt, on a par with the drug-pushers.

Sergeant Bulley's family consisted of three daughters. During his career and because of the nature of his work, he had come across some harrowing cases involving young women. This influenced his thinking, but also made home life a misery for the family. He had become intensely suspicious and over-protective, rarely allowing the girls out at night. No matter how well intentioned, this curfew became a double-edged sword involving bitter rows, with his long suffering wife caught in the middle. Delia, the twenty-one year old youngest daughter had rebelled and absconded with an elderly married man. This was the cause of a major upheaval in the house and resulted in Sergeant Bulley being absent from work for a considerable time. Some people suspected he suffered a nervous breakdown. This was never actually verified, but the rumour persisted. The incident also fuelled in

Sergeant Bulley a deep seated hatred of any old men he felt might be preying on young girls.

Garda Barry Moloney had a fair idea what his superior was like and felt it would be advantageous to be punctual and competent at his duties. In this he didn't disappoint, and as he strutted about the town the local people felt well advised to keep their distance. However, unknown to Sergeant Bulley, his new recruit was a complex individual, the complete and utter day-dreamer, possessing a vivid and colourful imagination. Unlike his contemporaries, he didn't involve himself in sport or frequent the pubs. Films were his number one hobby. He especially loved vicious, violent films involving the Mafia – with all the resulting mayhem. Other favourites were films where a renegade policeman, dispensing with protocol, meted out his own form of rough justice. As he walked the mean streets of Youghal he visualized himself as a plain-clothes cop, with a .45 Magnum in a shoulder holster tucked inside his sports jacket, known simply to all and sundry as Dirty Barry.

As he pounded the beat around the town he suddenly noticed two decrepit cars parked in a prohibited area. (When Nicky and Ned commented on how quiet their familiar parking area looked, both had failed to see the newly erected sign further down the street, stating "No Parking, Day or Night.") The little houses in the lane were deemed dangerous, were condemned, and the remaining couple of residents were finally relocated the previous week. In fact, one of the houses was already demolished. The road was due to be cordoned off completely. A new apartment complex was earmarked for the area.

On spotting the cars Barry's eyes narrowed, and he

felt a little exhilarated, knowing at last he had found something to occupy his mind. He reached eagerly for his official little black book and wrote in the time and date as he approached the cars. "Illegal parking," he wrote down, muttering,....'for a start.' He expressed amazement at the dirt on the bottom portion of both cars. He continued to write, "Registration plates illegible due to being covered by a thick film of dried clay and mud." He used the toe of his boot to remove the caked mud from the number plates.

At times, during a dry spell, Ned and Nicky used the cars to transport bales of hay and straw through the fields; hence the condition of the vehicles. "No tread on back left and front right tyres,' Garda Moloney observed, issuing a further prosecution. He moved next to Nicky's car which received the same treatment, except in this instance there was only one bald tyre. Looking in the windows he marvelled at how much junk the car contained — traces of straw and hay scattered about, discarded cigarette packets, sprockets, a broken fan-belt, a tractor filter, grease gun and pliers. Suddenly something more sinister caught his attention: moving his head sideways to get a better view, he satisfied himself that what he was actually looking at were the unmistakable double barrels of a shotgun — poking out from beneath a rug, on the back seat. (Explanation: two of Nicky's lambs had been killed and he had taken the gun with him, in case he came across the fox responsible. Returning to the car he had thrown the gun in the back seat, covered it with the rug and forgot about it.)

'This puts a different complexion on things,' Garda Moloney realized, whistling through his teeth. 'This could be serious.' Without hesitation he radioed back to the station. It wasn't long before Sergeant Bulley roared up in the squad car. Using modern computerized technology he quickly established the names and addresses of the two car owners. It was also confirmed that Nicky was the legal custodian of a shotgun, licensed for the control of vermin. Sergeant Bulley, though, felt there were questions to be answered: what was he doing in town with a concealed weapon? Garda Moloney's lucid imagination took flight, 'We'll contact the army, organize a controlled explosion, and blow this crock of shite to smithereens.'

'Hold on, hold on,' Sergeant Bulley admonished, 'this is Youghal; this isn't Beirut or Baghdad... What could he have the gun for?' he asked himself, out loud'

'A robbery!' Garda Moloney quickly ventured. 'Or violence against the person.'

'No, it's not robbery,' the sergeant assured him, 'not from the information I received. There could be some form of vendetta involved here – a row over property, maybe.' Through experience Sergeant Bulley knew that isolation, loneliness, alcohol dependence, depression and despair were sometimes responsible for elderly country people behaving in a dangerous, irrational manner. He was aware of a couple of fatal shootings lately, in disputes about land ownership. He glanced from one car to the other. 'Could be the two of them are after someone,' he surmised.

'You could be right there,' Garda Moloney agreed, his adrenalin pumping a little faster.

'I wonder is that gun loaded?' Sergeant Bulley pondered. He proceeded to try the door handles and, amazingly, one of the back doors was unlocked. 'Looks like he's careless,' the sergeant commented.

'Be careful, it could be booby-trapped,' Garda Moloney had cautioned.

'Don't be ridiculous!' Sergeant Bulley remarked. Putting on his gloves he reached in, gingerly released the mechanism and the gun snapped open. 'At least it's not loaded.'

By now a small knot of people had gathered at the entrance to the little street, wondering what was going on.

'New shoes, but what's this?' Sergeant Bulley observed, noting the brown, paper covered parcel, also concealed under the rug.

'Might be the cartridges?' Garda Moloney prompted.

'I'm not sure if this is ethical,' Sergeant Bulley murmured as he peeled away the paper covering. But then he knew that any action taken to allay public safety would be sanctioned automatically. As he opened back the brown paper he was confronted by the cover photo of Playboy – the nubile, naked form, of a young lady smiling up at him. On seeing this image Sergeant Bulley experienced a sudden metamorphosis. He flew into a paroxysm of fury, his hands trembled and his ruddy countenance assumed a purple reddish appearance. Four more, similar type, soft-porn magazines accompanied Playboy. 'Look at this filth!' he gulped out. 'Filth! Horrible degrading filth!' He paused as he struggled to compose himself... 'This is what they're selling nowadays.' He knew he had to control his emotions in front of Garda Moloney He steadied himself and took a few deep breaths.

Ever anxious to please, peering over the sergeant's shoulder, Garda Moloney remarked, 'Depraved, utterly depraved.' At the same time his mind momentarily flashed to his own cache of hardcore, hidden under the loose floorboard in his bedroom. Quickly the sergeant deposited the magazines back under the rug – as if fearful he might become contaminated merely by touch. Settling his cap, he backed out of the car and straightened up. 'This is a different matter now,' he announced. 'The men we're dealing with here could be a couple of perverts.'

'Sodomites,' Garda Moloney implied. 'Rapists maybe – or, more likely, a pair of paedophiles.'

'They must be interrogated,' Sergeant Bulley pronounced with vigour.

Equally animated, Garda Moloney concurred, 'Definitely, no doubt about it.'

'Yes, I'd like to have them two back at the station. There are questions to be answered. Important questions.'

'Undoubtedly. Guns and pornography – a lethal mix,' Barry confirms.

Just then, the Weasel Walsh, he of the bad teeth, the Patron Saint of Black's pub, joined the band of onlookers gazing down the street. Straight away he recognized Nicky's car – and Ned's, parked a bit behind.

'I'm confiscating this gun, for the time being, until we establish a satisfactory explanation,' Sergeant Bulley declared. Using his gloves, he reached in for the gun and took it back to the squad car.

On seeing this, one of the interested spectators intoned, with some awe, to a friend, 'Sergeant Bulley just foiled an armed robbery.' An alarmist opinionated further, 'Or a murder!' On hearing this The Weasel's lips curled back — like a dog waiting to fight – and he rubbed his hands together with glee. He couldn't wait to convey this remarkable news back to Black's

'They're probably in some pub,' Garda Moloney ventured. 'We might get 'em on the drink.' He noticed the intense look on the sergeant's face and, thinking back to the stories he heard, wondered was he about to get another turn.

'Maybe it appears I'm being personal about this, something that shouldn't happen, but I fear those two pose a threat to decent society, to the family way of life. They must be apprehended — that one in particular,' pointing to Nicky's car. 'It's for my own peace of mind, if nothing else. Are you with me on this one, Barry?'

'Oh all the way Sergeant.'

'That's what I like to hear.' He glanced at his watch. 'It could take a considerable length of time?'

'No matter. Even if it takes all night.'

'Good man. Look, I'll reverse the car down that little alleyway over there. You stand back into that doorway; make sure you're well concealed.'

'A kind of stakeout, Sergeant. Like you see in the films.'

'Well…. yeh, I suppose…a stakeout.'

'Pity we haven't guns. We should have.'

Sergeant Bulley scratched his head again, and he studied Barry, little questions beginning to nag at his mind.

Chapter Fifteen

Two Paupers

Back at McTaggart's lounge, Foxy is roughly swung about again before he finally extricates himself from Nicky's grasp. Ned is pleased that the table containing the drink remains intact.

'Hey boy, take it easy! Slow down.'

'You and your friggin' big mouth,' Nicky now growls. 'Blowin' about all the money you're earnin'. Fifty-five thousand a year! You're makin' us out to be two paupers. A bloody windbag that's all you are.'

'Christ, I only told the truth.'

'Wan thing, you didn't do our chances any good,' Ned implies.

Nicky supports this view, 'You banjaxed us.'

'I didn't know you had 'em in your sights.'

'Not alone are we paupers, but two thick ignorant paupers at that,' Ned emphasizes. 'You took the skids from under us, boy.'

'Hey, hold on. You've got it wrong. Look, they know the kind of men you are now. What would you be doing, huh? Puttin' on an act. They'd see through you right away. Women know about these things; it's a kind of instinct they have.'

'What are you sayin'? Who was foolin' who? Everything was straight down the middle,' Ned states.

'The kind of money we're earnin' will throw 'em out completely,' Nicky is now convinced. 'Christ, you had to draw that down, hadn't you.'

'Fifty-five thousand a year,' Ned spits out contemptuously. 'And the dole, bejasus.'

'Money isn't the problem here. You're barkin' up the wrong tree. I'm tellin' ye.'

Ned takes out a packet of cigarettes, puts one to his lips, then says, 'What am I doin'?' He returns the cigarette to the box.

'If I wasn't here what would you be talkin' about then? Well, come on, what would ye be talkin' about?'

'Plenty of things. Who the hell do you think you are?'

'We were getting' on fine till the two of you showed up,' Nicky reminds him. 'Why the hell didn't you shag off somewhere?'

'You'd be saying to each other things like, "How are the cattle doin' Nicky? Are you growin' any bit of corn this year?" "I don't know what to grow; them whores out in Brussels have the whole thing ruined with red tape. I might grow a bit of marijuana – it's the only crop there's any money in."'

'You know something, you're a bloody nuisance, that's all you are,' Nicky says with disgust.

'Foxy continues, 'They're out for the night. Women don't want to be talkin' about farmin' and things like that. Even Breda would want to leave it behind her.'

Ned is a little curious. 'Alright then, what do they want

to talk about?– seeing that you're such a smart arsehole.'

'Compliments!' Foxy now urges, attempting to make amends. 'Women love compliments. Even if they know you don't mean it, they still like to hear it.' He confronts Ned. 'Now Breda – and I hope you don't mind me saying this – looks a bit dowdy, with her hair and that, so you can't say too much. Tell her she have a great figure. And you know something, she would look really well if she went about it,' a fact he emphasises with passion.

'I know that.'

'I'd say that Nancy wan knows her way around the block.' He winks at Nicky. 'She'd suit you. I wouldn't mind chancin' her myself if things were different. Nicky, tell her that her hair is lovely, that you'd love to be somewhere alone with her so that you could run your fingers through it. Try to be a bit romantic, that's what the women like, boy.'

Nicky remains suspicious. 'You're just windin' us up again. Feck you now.'

'Christ, no, I'm not.'

'If we talked like that they'd think we were gone queer in the head,' Nicky concludes. 'Anyway, you heard her – about the lifestyle; she put her finger on it; she's not goin' to live on the side of a windswept hill.'

'You might regret this if you don't give it a shot. That's my opinion anyway. You don't get too many chances in this life. When you see an opportunity go for it. Feckin' go for it.'

'I'm sure you're worried what we do,' Ned intones.

'Grab your chance, don't hesitate.'

'Then there's this other fella, that she was mad about. Mark my words that man is still in her head and the divel in hell wont shift him,' Nicky surmises. 'Every twist and turn I'd make she'd be comparin' me to him.'

'I felt meself an' Breda were getting on okay, to be straight an' honest about it.'

'Good!' Foxy clenches his fist. 'That's the attitude to have. A bit of confidence is what it takes.'

'Twas only a feelin' now. I might be wrong. Hard to tell with a woman.'

'Oh yeh, you're right there.'

Nicky is weighing up the situation. 'Nancy now, I'd say, is twisting things around in her head, torturing herself over this man, wondering what went wrong.'

'Look at it this way', Foxy states, 'life is full of knocks and disappointments. I got plenty of 'em myself. That's life though, isn't it? You have to get on with it. Forget the past. The past can't be altered, the future can.'

Ned looks towards Nicky. 'Many's the kick in the guts we got down the years; wan more is not goin' to make much difference.'

'That's the spirit! For every old shoe there's an old sock.'

'You don't want to be kicked all over the place either,' Nicky implies. 'You can get that wan kick too many.'

As is his wont, Foxy puts his hand on Ned's shoulder, 'You tell Breda how safe she'd feel with a man around the house. And I'll tell you this for nothin', 'tis a hard old station on her, livin' there on her own.'

'Depending on a watch dog – guard dog, or whatever you'd like to call him.'

'A guard dog!' Foxy echos dismissively, stretching out his arm, 'Listen, fellows would come along with a bitch in heat, throw her over the wall and her guard dog would be gone off through the fields the same as if you tied a tin can to his tail.'

'It's tough on her alright, there on her own. Went from the fryin' pan into the fire like.'

'Some strange men walk the countryside by night. I saw some weird things boy, when I was out huntin' the foxes. The foxes aren't the only animals to come out when darkness falls.'

'Jasus, don't say that to her anyhow; don't frighten her.'

Nicky has reached a conclusion. 'I think the way we are is the way we're goin' to stay. That's my slant on it.'

Foxy points towards the hall. 'You'll soon know, they're comin' back.'

Chapter Sixteen

Decision Time

The womenfolk duly emerge up from the hallway. Nancy appears to have regained her composure and returns unassisted. If anything, she has an extra spring to her step.

Nicky holds out a chair. 'How are you now? Here, sit down.'

'Are you better?' Ned inquires.

I'm okay, I'm fine again. I felt a bit sick, that's all.' She quickly adds, 'I'm not drunk or anything.'

'We know that,' Nicky assures her. 'Oh God, that never entered the equation.'

'Mixing the old drink mightn't be the best,' Foxy remarks.

Ned agrees, 'That was it, I'd say.'

'That bottle of Port might be on the shelf out there for months – if not years.'

'We all have enough drink on board,' Trish announces.

'I made a fool of myself, didn't I?'

Nicky comforts her, 'No you didn't. What are you talkin' about?'

'Never again.'

'Ned consoles, 'Don't worry about it. Everything is okay, you're fine.'

'That finishes me with the drink. I never really liked it anyway. End of story.'

Trish sits back down. 'I had a tough enough day. Me legs are bet tonight. Late nights every night is killin' me.'

Nancy looks around. 'What we were talking about; I want you all to forget it, okay?'

'You're lucky to be rid of that guy,' Foxy says with conviction. 'Good riddance to bad rubbish is the way I see it.'

Breda, a bit sheepish looking, is standing to one-side.

'There must be a bad drop in that fella, a bad drop,' Nicky concludes.

'Put him out of your head girl, for once and for all,' Ned advises.

'Nicky monotones, 'Any man who'd do —-'

Nancy interrupts, 'For God's sake—!'

'Forget him, forget him,' Foxy says, putting his finger to his lips. 'Sssh, forget the bastard.' He brightens. 'Listen, we were talkin' while ye were down there.'

'No doubt you were. Well we were talking too,' Nancy emphasizes

Trish nods towards Nancy and Breda. 'They were talkin', I wasn't.'

Foxy continues, 'We were saying to ourselves it isn't good enough; that it's a hell of a lonely life for Breda, there on her own.'

'All that's going to change. Tell him, Breda.' Breda is hesitant. Nancy repeats, 'Go on, tell him.'

'Ned, we… we only met tonight, so I hope you wont mind too much. It's not as if we were going out together. You're not goin' to miss me…I mean…What I'm saying is, I'd rather not meet you again.'

Ned's face drops, and he goes a little pale. 'Oh! …you wont….you don't….I see.'

Foxy intercedes, 'Why? Heh, what's wrong with him? Christ, give him a fair crack of the whip. What's come over you?'

'It's the drink, mainly. I hate it. I have an aversion to it. Just look around you. Look at that table there.'

'He'll join the pioneers, he'll join the A.A., wont you?'

Ned sits down. 'Yeh….I will.'

'He'll join nothing! If we ended up together I know well what would happen.'

'You don't know. How would you know?'

'When the novelty wore off , he'd be at home nights, like a bear with a sore head, mad to go down to the pub. Eventually he'd go, and he'd keep going. I'd end up stuck at home, miserable, a lot worse off than I am now. That's what 'twould come to, nothing surer.'

'That's stupid talk. A man can change.'

'I was warned about it all my life. You know what my father often said? He often said, "marry a drunkard and you'll end up being a widow before he's dead at all."'
'You're probably an alcoholic, Ned, and you're not aware

of it.'

'No, you're wrong,' Ned responds in a low tone.

'If you don't mind me saying so, you should go for treatment.'

Foxy looks amazed, 'That's ridiculous talk. We're all alcoholics to you, I suppose?'

'I'd honestly say you are.'

'What!' He looks with astonishment to Nicky and Ned. 'Christ!, could you bate that?'

Breda stands beside and looks down at Ned. 'Look, you're a decent man. Wait and see, things will turn out all right for you yet. I'm only sorry things didn't work out different tonight. I just can't help the way I am. I just can't. You understand that, don't you?'

'I don't know. I thought we were makin' headway.'

'Breda, think careful now; you could be makin' a mistake,' Nicky proclaims.

Foxy supports this view, 'A big wan.'

Nicky continues, 'That's a sound man there; he'd look after you.'

'My mind is made up.' She again points to the table of mostly empties. 'Look at it. Just look at it.'

Foxy spreads his arms wide, 'We're havin' a social night out. The same as everybody else. Ned there could give it up like that,' he clicks his fingers.

Ned has his head lowered, 'Leave it now….leave it be.'

'I don't know what to say,' Nicky adds. There is a slight pause. He is standing behind Nancy. Hesitantly he starts to feel her hair. 'You know something, Nancy.'

'What?' She doesn't turn around.

'You have beautiful hair. What I'd love now, is to have you somewhere alone, where I could run my fingers through it.'

'Why don't you take off that silly hat, so that I can see have you any hair left that I can run my fingers through.' She laughs out loud. 'Jesus, do you hear him, Breda? He's getting romantic! Oh God! Him!'

Nicky feels mortified by her reaction. He turns away, blurting out gruffly, 'I'm just tellin' you! You have nice bloody hair.'

'Why, thanks. It's nice to...to...' She struggles to contain her mirth, 'to receive a compliment now and then.' She puts her hand to her mouth.... 'I'm sorry. Look, I don't know what you think of me, but as far as I'm concerned, I've had enough of men to last me a lifetime. I told you my situation, didn't I?'

'We're not all like him.'

'I know that. You're as different as chalk and cheese. Listen, we only met briefly, just by chance. What do you expect?'

'Short an' sweet, like an ass's gallop,' Nicky responds.

'That's what we are I'm thinkin' – two asses,' Ned's conclusion.

'Don't be talking like that. That's silly,' Breda says.

'Look, I'm sorry now –'

Foxy, unfazed, hasn't given up. 'You should grab the opportunity when it turns up. Meet 'em again, anyhow, do you hear me? Give 'em a fair chance. Maybe something like this wont happen to you again…. You'll be sorry you missed the boat.'

'He who hesitates is lost,' Trish contributes.

Nancy stands up. 'We know where you live if we change our minds.'

'Glentallagh,' Ned intones.

'We'll remember it.'

'Tell me something,' Foxy queries, 'what did you mean when you said things were goin' to change – with Breda there?'

'You know, we should be thankful for meeting you this evening. You helped us make a big decision.'

'Decision! What decision?'

I'm going to move in with Breda.'

All register profound surprise.

'What!' Nicky gasps.

'Move in with her? Live with her?' Foxy exclaims.

'Why not? Give me one good reason? It'll work out the finest. I'll have my wages, and in my spare time I'll help Breda out with the farmwork. We'll have each other. We'll be company for each other. That's the important thing.'

'It's a great idea, isn't it?' Breda enthuses.

'A great surprise I'd call it,' Foxy gulps.

'We're very compatible, you know,' Nancy informs, 'we both like the same things.'

'It looks that way,' Foxy sardonically agrees.

'What'll I hear next!' Nicky says, scratching his chin.

'Any good entertainment that's on in Waterford or Cork, or anywhere local, we'll go to it,' Nancy states.

Breda agrees. 'We've decided we're going to try and enjoy our lives. I didn't have much of that, up to now.' She points to Foxy. 'Like you keep saying – you only get the one chance.'

'That's why you should think again. Before it's too late. I'm tellin' you now.'

Nancy ignores him. 'Anyway, we had an interesting get-together. A bit on the short side, maybe.'

'I don't know what to make of ye now,' Nicky remarks.

'You left us down,' Ned murmurs.

'Breda implores, 'Don't be like that.'

'We were all strangers till a short time ago – weren't we?' Nancy states. 'No one is obligated to anyone. That's the way it is.'

'You've a long road ahead of ye, whether ye know it or not,' Trish declares. 'Are you sure you wont grow tired of each other?'

'We wont,' Breda is adamant.

'We know each other too well,' Nancy states.

Breda adds, 'Ned and Nicky are still friends after all those years.'

'They're not livin' together; not in the same house. Wait an' see.'

Nancy nods towards Nicky and Ned, 'I'd say you two fellows would find it hard to change your lifestyle now. Believe me, you're too set in your ways. You can't get an old dog off his trot – and that's a fact.'

'You think that, huh?' Nicky questions.

'Ned, it's like this,' she continues, 'if you had a woman on tow you'd feel trapped; your freedom would be curtailed.'

'Would it?'

'You'd be ringing up Nicky saying, "This house is like a prison, boy. Listen, the races are on in Listowel; we'll go down there before I go out of my mind. And we'll get pissed drunk while we're at it.'

Ned is not impressed. 'Different ways of lookin' at it. The house can become a prison alright.'

She looks about. 'Anyway, that's it, we'll be off... I have a sober driver an' all – no worries.'

Breda appears a bit crestfallen as she looks down at Ned. 'Ned, thanks for...for everything. It was really nice meeting you. You have my phone number so whenever you are down around our side be sure to call along. You'll be very welcome. I mean that.'

Without looking towards her Ned replies, 'Right, thanks.'

'Well…..goodbye so.' She goes out, giving a little wave of the hand.

'Goodbye then, Nicky,' Nancy now says. 'We had a few laughs anyway, didn't we?'

'Yeh. So-long.'

She crosses, glancing at Trish and Foxy. 'I'll probably see you two around the town.'

'Maybe,' Foxy mumbles.

'Heh!' Trish says.

Nancy turns round. 'Yeh?'

'Don't forget that job now.'

'I wont.' Nancy departs.

Ned looks around him, gesturing with his hands in futility, mingled with despair, 'Well, that's that.'

'That's fuckin' that alright,' Nicky rasps.

'Christ, that was some surprise.' Foxy shakes the head. 'It caught me on the hop, I'll tell you that.'

'Hey, listen, don't worry about 'em,' Trish says in a restrained tone. 'There's more fish in the sea, more pebbles on the beach. Don't let it get you down. Don't take it to heart, you hear me?'

Nicky grits his teeth, giving the table a thump in frustration. 'Nice hair you have! Laughin' at me. Christ! Fuck!'

'Gone to live together. Imagine that, huh,' Foxy now says with some disbelief. 'That came as a bolt from the blue.'

'Two feckin' idiots, that's what we are,' Ned says in a more muted, resigned tone of voice.'

Nicky is of like mind. 'Another kick up the arse. The same old story.'

'Twas all Nancy's doing,' Foxy is convinced. 'I'd bet money on it.'

Trish confirms: 'It was. That wan is a bit smart in herself. I don't think I'd be that struck on her. Maybe that other fella knew what he was doin'. There are two sides to every coin; you can be certain sure of it.'

Foxy looks a little tentative. 'Look, I'm sorry if you thought I put a spoke in your wheel. You know, I was only havin' the craic. I tried to square it for you, didn't I?'

'You weren't a help,' Ned responds. 'You cut close to the bone. Ridiculed us.'

'I did?'

'What difference,' Nicky concludes, 'twould have made no difference. We're not what they wanted. That's all there's to it.'

Trish wags the finger at Foxy. 'You'll be gettin' your nose flattened wan of these days. And it'll be your own fault. You're puttin' in for it.'

'I felt confident enough at first. I was only foolin' myself. An alcoholic, she said! Did you hear her?' Ned looks incredulous. 'An alcoholic! You'd think I was thrown down legless on the footpath.'

Nicky dismisses her opinion out of hand. 'She don't

know what she's talkin' about. How would she? Here, we'll have a feckin' drink. A good wan this time. I'm havin' a glass of malt.' He turns to Ned. 'And you?'

'The same. Might as well.'

Foxy moves forward. 'I'll get this wan.'

No, no, you wont. It's okay. Stay where you are.'

'Come on, come on, get out of my way.'

Nicky is resolute. 'I said no.'

'Come on, move over.' Foxy pushes Nicky aside.'

'Oh Christ, alright then, have it your way.'

'Shite, if you can't bate 'em join 'em,' Trish decides. 'I'll have the same.'

Foxy bangs on the hatch and gets a quick response. 'Four glasses of whiskey – Jameson', he orders. He looks around. 'Want anything through it?'

'No, there's water here.'

In a throw-away mode Foxy remarks, 'Probably in it already.'

'A dash of lemonade in mine,' Trish requests.

Foxy shouts through the opening, 'A drop of white lemonade in wan of 'em.'

With a weary shrug of the shoulders Nicky says, 'Another chapter in the book closed.'

'I'd say that's about the end of the book,' Ned rejoins.

'Forget 'em now,' Trish encourages.

'Not much else for it…Hopes dashed again.' Ned sighs, looking at his watch. 'The clock is movin' on. Maybe we'll doss down on the sofa tonight. Is that alright?'

'No bother,' Trish replies, 'Anytime. Didn't I tell you that?'

'Yeh, you did. Thanks.'

'They'll have a right old chin-wag goin' home now,' Nicky says with some rancour. 'Tomorrow the people around Dungarvan will know about the two idiots they met.'

'You're not idiots,' Trish assures him. 'Don't be talkin' like that. Have a bit of confidence in yourselves. There's nothing wrong with you. Nothing at all.'

Foxy fumbles in his pocket, locating a quantity of loose change, 'Here y'are'…He rummages some more and slams down whatever he has left on the counter. 'Here, have it all.' He turns, passing around the drinks, saying to Trish, 'This wan is yours.'

 'Thanks.'

Foxy automatically says 'Good-luck!' Nicky automatically responds likewise.

Ned intones, 'Good-luck, good-luck. We need some, I think.'

'Don't worry yourselves about them two', Foxy advises. 'Worse things could happen: you could fall off a roof or get run over by a bus. If you don't mind, I think I'll rest the pins for a bit. I suddenly feel as if I was hit between the ears with a lump-hammer.' He sits back, placing the whiskey on the table. He retains the cider bottle in his hand. There is a pause. Ned and Nicky are looking down at the floor.

Ned breaks the silence. 'You know I was growing to like her – Breda. Something about her. I thought, maybe tonight was goin' to be the start of something.'

'She looked different anyhow.' Trish rolls her eyes to heaven. 'Where in God's name did she get the clothes from? I wouldn't be seen dead in 'em.'

'Don't mind the clothes,' Ned says without thinking, 'it's what's inside the clothes that matters.'

'You know something,' Trish suddenly says, 'maybe you're as well off on your own, in the long run, when you come to think about it.'

Nicky looks up. 'Hey, Foxy!..Are you listenin'?...Heh, this is important…Are you listening?'

'Yeh…yeh.'

'Keep tonight to yourselves – both of you.'

'Christ, you know us better than that,' Foxy mumbles.

'You don't have to worry on that account,' Trish says fervently.

'I am worried. If they got wind of this at home in the pub we'd be done for.'

'They'd make our lives hell. We'd be laughed out of the place,' Ned confirms.

'I told you, don't worry about it.'

'If it gets out we'll know where it came from.'

'It wont get out.'

'Good, good.'

Trish muses, 'I wonder how will they get on? Over time, like? 'Twas Nancy's brainwave alright — 'twas she came up with the idea. I wouldn't say either of 'em will ever get hitched now.' She smiles. 'They don't need men. That's the right way to have ye.' The smile fades when she looks at their dejected faces. 'I'm only joking.'

Foxy stretches back in the chair and with a sleepy sounding voice says, 'Hey, Nicky.'

'What?'

'I wasn't in bed last night till four o'clock, but I was up on a roof this mornin' at a quarter past six.'

Nicky responds in a disinterested tone, 'You were.'

'As true as God.'

Trish stands over Ned and Nicky. 'You know what I was just thinking? There are a couple of girls I know, here in this town, who might take you two fellows on.'

Sounding sleepier still Foxy says, 'A quarter apast six, boy.'

'I have a couple in mind. Real honest-to-God, down-to-earth girls – well, women.' Ned and Nicky remain despondent, gazing down into their whiskey glasses. She continues. 'No fancy notions with 'em, or anything like that; know what I mean? Not like some of them snobs you'd see, goin' around with their noses cocked in the air thinkin' they're great. Not like your woman Breda either – there'd be a bit of life in 'em. I'll tell you this much, they'd be great for the craic, and they'd drink away all night with you – no bother. Well, what do you say? Will I put a word in for you? "If you don't chance your arm you wont break your leg."'

Nicky is unenthusiastic, to say the least. 'She said she had enough of men. I think we have enough of women, for the time being.'

Ned, too, is deflated. 'We'll keep our powder dry for awhile.'

'Please yourselves.' Pause. 'Maybe you're right. "Wance bitten, twice shy."' 'But sure, when you size it all up, aren't you fine the way you are. You can come and go as you please – no one to put in or out with you. Why go out and buy yourself trouble. Why buy a cow when you can buy a carton of milk. You know what I'm thinkin'; them two wans might turn out to be two right sergeant-majors yet. Maybe if you did end up with them two you might have no bit of comfort at all in life. Foxy there says some women can break a man's spirit – the same as you'd break-in a horse.'

'I suppose,' Ned says, his mind elsewhere.

'There's no "supposin" about it. I could name several from around here who were changed men wance they got married. The smiles melted from their faces. Petticoat government took over.' She wags the finger again. 'What I mean is, you have to have fair-play all round. Give an' take, that's my policy. It's the only way. Do you get me meanin'? But when there's only wan trousers, and the woman hops into it, watch out.'

Foxy has dozed off. His hand, holding the cider bottle

has gradually tilted over so that the liquid spills on to his thigh, and down on to the floor. Trish spots this. She goes over and gives the sole of his runner a good kick. Startled, he reacts, jumping up, spluttering, 'What the!...?'

'You're spilling the stuff,' she admonishes.

'Christ!' he exclaims, brushing himself down.

'That's lovely. You pay for it, then spill it all over the floor. How much money have you left now? Feck all.'

'Money….money! It's always money with you. I have plenty of it.' He takes a wad of notes from his pocket. 'Look.' He nods his head. 'That was only change.'

'Tomorrow is shopping day for us.'

'Good…money…Money!' Suddenly he is sharply alert. 'You just reminded me of something!' Enthusiastically he goes and shakes Nicky by the shoulders. 'Heh, listen! It's just come to me. Out of the blue! Out of the sky!'

'What? What's wrong with you?'

'The solution to all your problems. It just hit me!'

'What are you on about?' Ned also is suddenly attentive.

'What are you sayin'?' Trish says irritably.

'The answer to your prayers.'

'What?'

'Sites, boy, sites!'

'Sites,' Nicky repeats.

'Buildin' sites! Christ, you'd make a fortune. A bloody fortune!'

Lethargy all gone, Nicky and Ned are on their feet.

'I never thought of that,' Nicky exclaims, eyes wide.

'Never!' Ned gulps, adrenalin suddenly pumping.

Trish is now also excited. 'There you are! That's it. Now you see.' She holds her hands up in front of her face in an ecstatic fashion.

'Ned, listen, you own the land down that straight stretch of road, don't you? Nicky's on the other side – the boreen an' all?'

'Yeh, that's it,' Ned confirms.

'Sites! You're in the money now. You're in it in a big way,' Trish exclaims.

'What's a site worth?' Nicky asks.

'A fortune! A feckin' fortune up there. Let me see.' He scratches his forehead. 'With that view, you'd get close to a hundred and fifty thousand for half an acre.'

'What!' Ned gulps. You're jokin' me!' He appears as if he's in a state of collapse.

'Holy God!' Trish exclaims. 'Are you listenin' to that?'

'That much?' Nicky queries. 'Are you sure?'

'I'm tellin' you!'

Looking upwards, Ned crosses himself. 'God, You're up there after all.'

Foxy punches the air. 'You're made up. You're in the big league – the big money league.'

Trish enthuses. 'They're mad lookin' for sites, all over

the place. Aren't they? You're always sayin' it?'

'They're cryin' out for 'em; they're desperate for 'em; they're not makin' 'em anymore.'

'Christ above!' Nicky gasps. He points to his chest. 'Me heart is pumpin' like a clock gone wrong.'

'Cork City, Cork Port, Cork Airport – no distance; the towns all round, the sea, everything. Builders would give their right arm for that land. If the right man came along would you sell?'

'Sell!' Nicky declares loudly, 'I'd take the arm straight from the shoulder.'

Ned also confirms. 'For that kind of money who wouldn't? You're not havin' us on?'

'No. The two of you are millionaires.'

'Millionaires ...' Nicky looks at Ned. 'Millionaires....Us two.'

Trish is beaming, hands held wide. 'Now you see. I always say it – "behind every cloud there's a silver lining."

'You'd still have enough land left to keep you occupied. A few pedigree cattle, something like that.'

Ned expands, 'A kind of hobby, like all the big shots.'

'Nicky is also enthralled. 'A horse or two, maybe.'

'Nicky boy, like myself, you were always fond of the ponies.'

Trish elaborates. 'You've hit the jackpot – the same as if you won the lotto. I told you he'd come up with something.'

'Foxy you're a genius,' Nicky says. 'I always said it.' He looks at Ned again. 'Didn't I always say it?'

Ned points out warily. 'There was a man inquiring about that land alright. He wanted to know who owned what. I gave nothin' away though. I didn't like the cut of him.'

'Was he a big whore, with a fat belly and a red beard?'

'Yeh, that's him.'

Foxy emphatically waves his finger. 'Christ, keep a mile away from that rogue, that whore, that gangster. Fellas like him are only out to screw you. That's what you're up against. Listen, leave it to me. I'll see you right. I know the business, I know the ropes boy.'

'He knows it inside out. Leave it to him. He'll handle it for you, don't worry.'

Nicky faces Ned. 'We're sittin' on two goldmines. Put it there.' He holds out his upturned palm and Ned slaps it in the traditional "fair-day" manner.

Foxy glances eagerly from one to the other and then, in a conspiratorial manner says, 'You know what we'll do, the four of us? You know what we'll do?— we'll go on a holiday. And you know where we'll go?'

'Where?' Nicky asks.

'Lisdoon,' Ned suggests.

'No. Thailand!' Foxy states triumphantly.

Nicky is euphorically carried away. 'Thailand, yes! Yes! If Jonny McNulty could get a woman out there so can we.'

Ned's smile is huge, 'Why not!'

Trish is in heaven. 'Oh God, oh God, that's what we'll do. We'll all head off.'

'Soon as we sell the first site,' Nicky declares.

'No more Bluebirds or Hillman Hunters,' Foxy exhorts.

Ned holds his hands out wide. 'Gather round. Come on, come on.' They entwine their arms around the shoulders, forming a circle. Ned commences to sing:
'Come on boys and you'll see, lads and lassies in their glee.'
(All join in with gusto)
'Evergreen bowers would make your heart thrill,
The boys they will not harm you,
The girls they will all charm you,
Here's up 'em all says the boys of Fairhill.'

Foxy interrupts, shouting, 'The third verse — Gurranabraher. He starts the singing this time. The others quickly join

'Come on boys around by Gurranabraher,
'Tis there you'll see the fields so green,
The sun shines in splendour the lark sweetly sings,
Thousands come from o'er the foam,
Just to kiss the Blarney Stone,
You can view it all alone from the groves of Fairhill.

Come on boys and spend the day,
With our hurling club so gay,
The clash of the ash it would make your heart thrill,
Talk about the Kerry pike,
Let them all come if they like,

They're bound to be knocked out by the boys of Fairhill.'

They clatter their feet on the floor as they dance about ecstatically. Foxy shouts, 'Yahoo!'

Epilogue

About four miles from Youghal, on the Dungarvan road, Breda and Nancy have pulled over, into a lay-by. Back in the distance the flickering lights of the town are still visible. Nancy has removed her coat and the low neckline of her blouse reveals her ample bosom. She has finished smoking a cigarette and flicks the butt-end out the window.

'Does the smoking annoy you?'

'No, I don't mind.'

'Providing I don't blow the smoke up in your face. I noticed you turning away. I'll have to give 'em up; that's a sure thing. Listen, anything I do that might annoy you tell me, wont you? – any little thing at all. I mightn't be aware of it. No use in irritating each other.'

'The same with you. There are probably things about me?'

'Nothing I can think of straight away, but seeing that we'll be living together it would be nice to have everything sorted out – even the teeny-weeny small things.'

'When are you moving down?'

'The sooner the better. Is tomorrow evening okay?'

'Yeh, terrific.'

'A couple of suitcases should do the trick. Clothes, that's all.'

'Breda exhales deeply, 'God above, I never thought the

night would end like this.'

'Me neither. I feel exhilarated now,' Nancy happily exclaims. 'I feel excited and wonderful. I suddenly feel free – of everyone.'

'So do I,' Breda responds intensely.

'Are you sure?... Really sure?' Nancy asks, studying Breda's face.

'Yes.'

Nancy puts her arms around Breda, hugging her close. 'We'll always have each other from now on. No one will ever come between us.'

'We'll never be lonely again.'

'Never.'

'We're going to have a great life, aren't we,' Breda probes, seeking further assurance.

'We are. We can make it that way. Everybody needs warmth and affection in life. We're going to have that.' She squeezes Breda's hand.

A police car suddenly approaches, slows down and pulls in, headlights beaming.

'What do they want?' Nancy whispers, a little apprehensively, rolling up the window, settling back into her seat.

'We're alright,' Breda says. 'Everything is okay. I'm sober remember?'

After a few seconds the police car swings around and moves away.

'You see,' Nancy says, relieved, 'no one bothers two women. That's the way it's going to be.'

'They check everything, don't they?'

'Seems that way. It's a good thing, maybe.'

'I suppose.'

'I'd have got some fright if I was sitting in your seat. Woh! How silly it could happen.'

'Yeh.' There is a slight pause.

'Will people talk about us?' Breda asks, reflectively.

'I don't give a fiddler's!' Nancy retorts vehemently. 'I'm not going to worry about what people think anymore. Do you care?'

'Twas bred in me, to worry, I think. At first, maybe I will, to be honest.'

'Well don't. What are we doing wrong? Answer me that?'

'Nothing. You're right.'

'They'll comment about it; they'll say this an' that. But after a short time it'll be accepted. The oul' fella will fly off the handle alright. Oh God, I can picture him. There'll be high-jinks. Don't be even surprised if he arrives along to the house.'

'Would he? He'd never?'

'Don't worry about him. I'm well able to put him in his place.'

'The less bother the better.'

'It might be a good thing. He'll learn to appreciate my mother a bit more. That man couldn't even boil an egg for himself.'

Breda turns and looks back towards Youghal. 'I wonder are they still back there in the pub?'

'They'll be there till they're thrown out.'

'I suppose. You know, in a way, I feel a bit sorry for Ned. He was sound enough – only for the problem he has…. An innocent kind of person. I feel a bit guilty. Maybe he feels I led him along.'

'You didn't. How could he think that? That's being silly.' She laughs. 'Did you notice the red noses on the pair of 'em? They reminded me of two red-nosed reindeer.' She giggles again, 'Did you ever see anything as sudden as Nicky? Christ above, the very first time we met! That man is really desperate for a woman – any woman who'd cross his path. He reminds me of an old bull puckin' the ground. All he's lacking is a ring in his nose.'

'The night, 'twas all a bit unusual.'

'They were something alright – the four of 'em. I'd say they hit the bottle the whole time. All the money they must spend. I'll tell you one thing, I wouldn't like to be alone in a dark room with that Foxy fella.'

Breda smiles, 'Or Nicky – from what you just said.'

'Oh God, worse still! Did you hear him – about the hair? Imagine him pawing at you.' Nancy, herself now, gently strokes Breda's hair. 'Will we go home?'

'Yes, we'll go home …home.'

Breda starts up the engine and they edge out on to the road.

'There's a whole new life stretching out ahead of us,' Nancy says, 'a whole new beginning.'

....

It is well past the official closing time at Bobby Black's pub. The door is shut and bolted. Jimeen the Rat is the only customer left on the premises. Bobby is complaining away, in his usual fashion, as he sweeps up the floor. 'People are drinking more at home now. The foreigners, I'd say, introduced that trend. The "drink driving" and the cigarette ban have us all destitute. Wine, now, a lot of the young people are drinkin'. Did you ever think you'd live to see the day. I remember when real men used say that wine was only fit for washing your teeth.'

'If things are that bad,' the Rat says, 'how is it that pubs make such huge money when they're put up for auction? Answer me that?'

'That's only in the cities and large towns, boy. The country pub is in trouble; the country pub is bet.'

'Be Christ, you're not bet anyhow. Look at the crowds you had over the weekend. There's no fear of you losing sleep over your finances. You! Sure you have bits of land in near the town an' all. Worth a fortune.'

'I have to think of the family. It's hard going.'

'Like hell 'tis hard goin'. Bobby Black, you're an oul' moaner, you know that? I'd have no sympathy for you, and you might as well know it. I'd have more sympathy for the old black cat sitting on his arse outside on the window ledge.'

'People don't have sympathy for publicans. That's a known fact. What about the long hours we put in? Waiting on people like yourself.'

'Oh be God, you'll have me feeling sorry for you next. The tears are starting to roll down my cheeks already. Why don't you sell up and move out to Mauritious or somewhere? Get yourself another woman. She'd do you the world of good.'

A coin is heard tapping a few times on the front window. They pause and cock their ears. The rat-tat-tat is repeated.

'That's the Weasel's knock,' the Rat announces. 'You better lave him in. Give him wan.'

'What a life,' Bobby comments as he crosses to open the door. He'd love to tell the Weasel and the Rat to take a flying jump into the nearest river. Economics, however, dictated otherwise. Only the other day he calculated that the Rat, on average, left him eighty euro a week profit. That's over four thousand a year. Not to be sneezed at. The Weasel—even allowing for bad debts, like the drinks he gets on the slate that will never be paid for – leaves him, roughly, sixty euro a week profit. Every cent the Weasel can lay his hands on goes over the counter. Bobby Black is aware that the Weasel and the Rat are his two best customers.

The door is opened and the Weasel scurries in, rubbing his hands together. 'That's great! It's great to be home,' he gasps. I had to walk nearly half-ways from Youghal. The feckin' motorists wont pick you up anymore. What's gone wrong?'

'They'd be well off pickin' you up,' the Rat says, 'and you staggering all over the road. 'Tis a miracle to me how you're still alive.'

'I'm as sober as a judge.' He nods his head in a confidential way at the whiskey bottle. He nods again to indicate that payment will be made in due course. Bobby pours him a measure of whiskey.

'Anything new?' The Rat queries.

'New! Be God, you can be sure I have. Wait'll you hear this.' With glass in hand, back to the counter, the Weasel excitedly regales the others with his story about Nicky Daly, the guards and the gun. Using expletives as adjectives he exaggerates the tale out of all proportion. Bobby Black, being tactful, never wanting to become embroiled in anything that might be construed as controversial, walks towards the other end of the bar, commenting en-route, 'That's a terror.' He winks at Jimeen the Rat. 'Ah there must be some explanation – sure we all know Nicky.' Jimeen listened attentively. However, knowing well the way the Weasel embellished his stories – the reference to Mountjoy Jail an indication – he wasn't overtly impressed. None-the-less, he decided to buy the Weasel a drink. He knew that's what he was wangling for in the first place. A juicy story expected a reward. 'Give him a pint,' he instructs Bobby.

'Oh God above look down with pity on me,' Bobby balefully murmurs in despair.

Feeling like one himself the Rat instructs him further, 'Make that two. We'll drink 'em down in a flash; we'll be gone in a minute.'

'Oh you will.'

'We will. I'm beginning to feel a bit tired, to be honest. Old age must be catchin' up on me.'

'What do you think of all that?' the Weasel asks the Rat.

'It's a good wan alright. We'll wait an' hear his side of the story.' He turns away. 'Heh, Bobby, do you know the definition of old age? Old age is when an associate tells you he admires your new alligator shoes when, in actual fact, you're barefoot.'

. . . .

It is two-thirty in the early morning as Trish, Foxy, Ned and Nicky finally make their boisterous way back to the little house on the outskirts of the town. Ever so often Ned blasts out "The Banks of My Own Lovely Lee," in his loud, nasal, unappealing singing voice. Windows open and shut, and angry, sleep-interrupted people shout things like, "Go home be damned or I'll call the guards!" Or, "Shut up, you drunken tramps!" They don't care, as they are buoyed up with promises of undreamed of riches.

Arriving at the house Trish puts on the kettle to make the tea, and a pound of sausages are soon sizzling on the frying pan. By mutual consent they decide to take tomorrow – meaning "today" – off. They would celebrate their new found good fortune by going on the piss all day. Foxy is adamant that they use a taxi to ferry them around to the various watering holes. 'On no account,' he says, 'would any of them get behind the wheel of a car. No way!' he stresses vehemently. 'It takes twelve hours or more, to get the alcohol out of the system. Did any of you know that?' he asks importantly, looking around. 'I bet you didn't. Bulley, or that new fecker could nail you. 'No,' he warns, tapping his forehead, 'we'll use our loaves.'

Enjoying the fry, Foxy announces that when the Eskimos have guests, as a gesture of friendship, they share their womenfolk. On that basis he suggests that Nicky and Trish hop into the double bed for the night. Nicky stares at him, mouth agape, not knowing whether he is serious or what. Unimpressed, Trish chases Foxy around the table, a high heeled shoe held in her hand, threatening to kill him. Ned produces a half bottle of whiskey from his inside pocket. He starts to sing again but is quickly told, in no uncertain terms, to shut up, that he can't sing.

Nicky says that he'll have to ring Daddy in the morning with some excuse as to why he wont be going home. With alcohol induced gaiety they laugh over what Nicky will say. Cruel suggestions are made as to where Paddy could stick his crutch. Finally, through Foxy's main prompting, they decide on the following. As a memory help, he scribbles it down:

"Daddy, I can't go home today. Something extremely urgent has turned up, so I'll be unavoidably detained. I have an appointment with the chairman of the County Committee of Agriculture, to discuss reforms to the Common Agricultural Policy. As you know, red tape and bureaucracy have got completely out of control. (Foxy has a dictionary in one hand which he consults frequently)

Something needs to be done urgently about it and I, Nicky Daly, personally, am going to see to it that something is done. The chairman informed me that I might also be requested to go to Brussels to represent a new farming organization that has been founded called The Hardy Hill Farmers of Europe. As you can understand, this is a signal honour, not to be overlooked. Destiny is beckoning. Anything you need to eat is in the fridge. I know you'll be alright till I get back. I'll be with some very, very important people today so I can't put a timeframe on when exactly I will be home. The best attitude to adopt is to expect me when you see me. Don't forget to say a prayer for me, that everything goes alright."

'Well, what do you think of that?' Foxy concludes, looking about.

Nicky laughs, 'He'll know well I don't talk like that. A county councillor couldn't make that up better.'

Between giggles, Trish says, 'Paddy will be proud of you Nicky.'

'Or he'll think I'm gone stark ravin' mad altogether, heh-heh-heh,' Nicky laughs. 'He'll be sendin' for the men in the white coats.' He laughs some more, as do the others. 'I'll make up something that he'll understand.'

It doesn't take long before all are overwhelmed by a deep desire for sleep. Nicky is soon curled up on the sofa, comatose. Ned is rolled up in a ball, on the spare bed, snoring something awful. Foxy is spread out on the double-bed, a contented expression on his face, having being transported to dreamland: he is stretched back on a deckchair, on a beach in Thailand, surrounded by a bevy of female beauty, a large, cool cocktail in his hand. Trish, too, is in that strange land of dreams. A happy smile is dancing on her features: she is dressed all in white, on her father's arm, walking slowly up the aisle of the local church. The organ is playing "Here Comes the Bride." Foxy steps out to greet her. The priest, smiling benevolently, beckons them forward.

·········

The town clock tolls three-thirty a.m. Garda Barry Moloney is still hunched up in the doorway. As it tends to do in Ireland, the weather has changed dramatically. The early morning has turned extremely cold down by the waterside. A sudden blanket of frost has enveloped the town. Unfortunately Barry is wearing his light summer uniform. His lips have turned blue and his teeth start to chatter. The previous evening's enthusiasm has long since vanished. This has turned out to be one of the worst nights he has ever had to endure. He is in a vile mood right now. He feels Sergeant Bulley should have called this whole thing off hours ago. He should have impounded those cars, or got clamps somewhere and clamped them. The stupid clown should have done something. He curses his luck for ever having joined the Garda Siochana. He swears he will resign and apply to join the cops in New York. He might get assigned to Homicide. There are a few people he'd like to shoot right now. Inwardly he swears about a lot of things. He reserves his choicest language for Sergeant Jim Bulley.

There are few secrets in a garda station, and Barry was well informed about the sergeant's daughter and the effect the incident had on the sergeant himself: how he had became obsessive and developed a phobia about elderly married men whom he felt had designs on young women. How he began to monitor the behaviour of certain men in the town – among them some prominent business men. This didn't, or hasn't, gone down too well. Pretty soon the grapevine had it that Sergeant Bulley was a wee bit mentally deranged. Next it was whispered that he prowled the streets of the town after dark, peering through windows. His suitability for the post is currently being investigated. Garda Moloney draws back his leg and kicks the wall. 'Why must I have to suffer over the sergeant's fanaticism! Christ! Talk about lunatics runnin' the asylum!' He kicks the wall again, a little bit too hard this time, and he hops about on one leg.

Sergeant Bulley is still seated, in a stooped position, in the garda patrol car. He, too, is feeling the chill. He has retrieved an old worn garda overcoat from the boot of the car and has this wrapped around him. He has his beads out and is well into his fourth rosary, beseeching Divine Intervention to deliver unto him the drivers of those two automobiles. The remaining denizens of the town of Youghal are fast asleep in their beds. .... Goodnight.

REDFERNE